Whatever You Cherish

by
Ava Coffier

Copyright © 2015 by Ava Coffier

First Printing: 2015

ISBN 978-0-9940950-0-8

www.avacoffierauthor.com

www.avacoffierauthor.com

Acknowledgements

I would like to thank my editor, Marisa Pellegrino for putting her whole heart and soul into editing this project. It wouldn't be the same without her!

I would also like to thank my husband, family and friends for supporting me through this whole process.

Thank you. Without your support and patience, I would have never achieved my dream

Dr. Robeline

The room was hot and potent with the smell of eucalyptus. It drove me insane; all I could think of was the itchy feeling on my palate. Although the scent cleared my sinuses, I found myself gagging on the dry air. I crossed my legs and waited in forced patience. I tried to ignore the clicking of the vents and focus on the mute hum of the room. Nothing was better than silence.

Talking was endless in this place and it was getting on my nerves. All I really needed was to reflect on myself. I didn't need to mull over my problems and discuss what had happened. Talking was a problem in and of itself for me. I always found the wrong things to say. Most of the time I didn't mean the brutality of my words, but whatever I said seemed to come out the wrong way. Like my words were tumbling out and I didn't know how to organize them in an orderly fashion.

Shuffling my feet, I stared at my black fabric flats. I had them for too long; the sole was beginning to come off. My left foot picked at the exposed sole, flipping it back and forth, back and forth, back and forth. Tick-tock-tick-tock.

1

Suddenly the door swung open behind me and someone strode in. Pressing my back into the chair, I took a deep breath, nerves catching fire all over my body. Although I was anticipating that moment, the sound of the door slamming made me jump in my seat.

I glanced out the window and wished I were anywhere but in that cramped room, suffocating with anxiety. It was mid fall. I hoped winter would come early.

Every time the season changed, it held some magic for me; it was the promise of a new beginning. Except this time, that wasn't really the case. I had to deal with my demons. It was time to face my problems and even though I was aware of that, I wished I could shrivel up and float out the screen of the half-opened window.

Tearing my gaze from the orange, red and yellow trees outside, I glanced at the dark haired women across from me. She was shuffling objects out of a bag. Number one, a notebook, then a blue pen, then sugar packets, which she promptly ripped open and added to her coffee that was sitting to her right. The aroma of black coffee travelled to my nose and I drank it in. I would have killed for a strong coffee.

"Hi, I'm Doctor Robeline," the women extended her long,

thin hand out to me and smiled, revealing yellowing teeth in the corners of her mouth. Gross. Her dark hair was tied back neatly in a ponytail. Very professional. Her eyes were too close together and beady, however, her skin was clear. She might have been attractive at one point in her life but it looked like she had too many sleepless nights and drank too much coffee because of a caffeine addiction. But who was I to judge.

"I'm Ivy," I said, shifting my gaze away from Robeline as soon as I spoke.

It was too much too feel her eyes on me, studying me, looking over my appearance and making assumptions. It made me uncomfortable. It was the type of uncomfortable that made me forget how to speak English, or to walk straight without tripping over my feet.

Even though I convinced myself I didn't care about what people thought of me, it still scared me that this woman that I didn't know just might hate me or dissect me in the same way I did her. Then again, I knew that that thought wouldn't serve me anything. She was my doctor, she was supposed to help and I wasn't supposed to feel judged by someone I would unload all my thoughts and feelings onto.

Rationality of the situation always seemed to come afterwards. That was arguably part of my problem, but then again, I wasn't in any place to diagnose myself; hence the doctor that was peering across the table at me with curiosity.

Robeline raised her light brown, (obviously) penciled-in eyebrows. "Well Ivy, do you want to tell me a few things about yourself to get us started?"

I stared at her penciled eyebrows, trying to find the words to say but I couldn't get past her hypothetical question. Of course I didn't want to tell her about myself. I didn't even want to be there. Holding eye contact, I stared at Robeline with a blank expression. I wasn't in the mood to dive into a deep discussion about myself. As if that wasn't clear enough.

I was lost. There wasn't much I would say about myself anyway. I would have rather got right to the subject. It was all I could think about. Although my story was messed up beyond belief I knew I had to get it out. It was time to sort it out. If anyone could help me, it was Robeline.

Running my tongue over my canine tooth, I cringed at the startling silence that grew over the room, multiplying by the second.

After shifting in her seat Robeline took a deep breath and

dove in to uncomfortable conversation. "The whole idea of telling each other a little about ourselves is to get warmed up and then we can start talking about what happened. I don't expect you to unload it all on me right away, but I do expect some progress so we can keep the process moving smoothly," she paused to sip her coffee, not breaking eye contact and freaking me out with her intensity. "Is that alright?"

I leaned back into my chair. It was probably too rude to just tell her to get on with it. And I was working on my patience so that wasn't an option.

Robeline stared at me for a moment before shifting her eyes away from me. "Okay I'll begin," Robeline said. She bared a wide smile as if compensating for starting off on an awkward note. It was too enthusiastic. "I love to paint and camp with my family but my real love is helping people. I was born in Ohio but moved around a lot as a kid. I didn't have much of a social life when I was young. I met my husband in college and we decided to move out here to Golden to settle down and have a family. We wanted the serenity and quietness of a small town. And then I found this job and I've been here ever since." She smiled delicately, as if she had given me her whole life story in a jumbled, thoughtless mess and now it was my turn.

I wanted to laugh in her face. Met her husband in college, has a passion for painting and helping people. I mean, come on. This was so cliché and sharing such 'in depth' information about ourselves was completely unnecessary. Nor did this make me trust her any more. The only thing that made me even want to talk to this women was the PhD hanging on the wall behind her head. But of course it was too 'abrupt' to just say that.

Stiffening my jaw, I stared at her. "I'm not going to participate in mindless small talk, I came here to talk about what happened," I paused, "And even that is too long of a story."

"We have time," Robeline assured me. Her lips bended into a tense smile; an attempt at kindness that didn't touch her dark eyes. I could tell she was irritated by my response and she was a bad actor.

I wondered how many clients she had and how many times she pretended to care about her patients. She had likely been through a hundred or more in her lifetime. I sympathized for her, only because it would be exhausting to have to be nice over and over again. To pretend to care was hard enough as it was. Even then, I couldn't help but be angered by her fake response. It made me want to punch her in her yellowing teeth.

6

"I'm aware," I said, scowling. My thumb found it's way to my mouth and subconsciously, my teeth ripped at the edge of the nail that was already bitten down to a stub. Pain stung through my nail and I regretted letting my nerves take over.

"Well," Robeline said, "If you don't want to introduce yourself outright, do it as you tell me about Alana."

Her name rang hollow through my mind. I swallowed and tried to ignore the goose bumps that rolled from my neck down to my wrists.

Chewing the inside of my lip, I leaned forward and tried to shrug off every part of me that was telling me to turn around and leave. Ignoring the butterflies whirling and crashing in my stomach, I started to explain the problems I had before everything went to absolute hell.

~

There was something about Alana's smile. Dashing would be the most accurate word to describe it. Whenever she smiled, she seemed to cock her head to the side a little, as if lost in thought. Her eyes were part of the smile, radiating through her as if she were hysterically happy for a flickering moment. I couldn't even begin to explain the feeling that her smile gave me. It made me feel like I was worth something, even if it were for something stupid like being humorous or sarcastic. Since I had little to no self-esteem, it gave me a sense of purpose when I made her happy, although it rarely happened. I didn't make Alana happy; I enraged her more than anything. So much for sisterly love, if that was ever really a thing.

Alana was older than me by two years. She was gorgeous and lively. She was the most put-together person I had ever met. She was the closest thing to perfection. She had stunning clothes and a quirky personality. Everyone seemed to be intrigued by her. She had long blond hair that fell down to her waist and beautiful light blue eyes that would light up when she spoke out of excitement. Her eyes revealed so much about her. I could read every emotion of hers from the light in her eyes. I could tell if she was lying, angry or faking a smile.

She carried a bizarre energy; it was so alive. She had a hearty laugh and an incredible sense of shamelessness; she was who she was and she held a sense of dignity for being different. I guess that is what we all want - to be something special. For her, it just came naturally. I couldn't help but question why she was who she was and why I was so different. I figured she just won the gene-lottery.

We lived in Golden. Alana had her hobbies. She was big into snowboarding and dreamed of being in the Olympics; she had ambition to say the least. We lived with our grandparents because our parents had died in a car crash when we were just 8 and 10. We lived a life of normalcy, despite the fact that half of our family was crushed in an accident. I tried not to let it bother me; I didn't even seem to remember my parents anyway. Alana remembered them better.

Alana was getting ready to go to University and I was fresh out of high school. My name is Ivy. I was always the shadow of my sister's perfection. I was the opposite of her; I was gawky and awkward with mousy brown hair that spiraled in tight curls and fell to my shoulders. My eyes - brown. I wore bland awkward clothes that made me look awful and I had absolutely no sense of style. I had no urge to better myself physically, emotionally or mentally, even though I knew I needed improvement. In fact, I couldn't stop thinking about how much I needed to do to save myself.

I was never popular. I was the kid in the library at lunch and on breaks in our old high school. An outcast, I found myself buried into books for an escape. When I left high school, I left all my "friends" behind as well. Turned out the only thing we had in common was high school, that and the fact that we didn't have any friends because most of them were just as hateful towards social interaction as I was. Most people labeled me as "weird." They all wondered how Alana and I were related. So did I.

Even though I thought I was secure with myself and that Alana was just something that I could never be, I always wished I was her. Of course there was more to her life than what I would know. She did cast a large web of lies that seemed impossible to keep up with. It still would have been easier to switch places with her. Alana had an easy life. She was someone who had everything. She was a somebody. She had it together. She had dreams and ambitions and hobbies, and to top it off she was going to school to be a doctor – that was if the Olympics didn't work out for her. Alana had the determination that I would never have.

My situation was similar to that of an engine cutting out on a ferris wheel, just as I got to the top. I hated those things enough as it is. How the hell would I have been dragged onto it? Who knows, but being at the top was enough to make my breath halt in my throat and my heart to quicken against my ribcage. I lacked the courage to climb down because every time I looked down, I realized I was not capable of climbing. All I could picture was my sweaty palms giving out on the bars on my way down. Hell, how would I even climb out of the stupid basket that kept swinging in mid air with ever gust of wind? I felt safer with my palms sweating and my heart giving out. I felt safer not being able to breath, with the possibility of passing out and maybe finding something better in my dreams. I lived my life in fear. I was scared not moving, but I was incapable of changing that.

Alana's boyfriend, Matt, seemed to love her to no end. I envied her because of how much he did just to linger in her presence. He was the perfect boyfriend, starting with his stunning looks of dirty blond hair and blue eyes. He had a smile that held so much goofiness that even looking at him made me smile. He knew Alana had a light in her and he was just as attracted to it. So much so, he wanted to have her forever. I would die for that type of love.

Alana made up for what I didn't have; in fact she excelled at what I didn't have. She had a perfect boyfriend, whom she took advantage of. She had any guy she wanted and I couldn't even get a guy to glance in my direction and pretend I was female. I would never have a love like that, it simply didn't happen for people like me. I wasn't perfect. I didn't have a light in me.

Alana had life at her fingertips, she even radiated with it. Of course, she had to ruin that because she didn't seem to notice how fortunate she was. And here begs the question; why do the lucky ones always mess up their lives? Maybe it was boredom but for whatever reason, Alana didn't seem to care how lucky she was to have someone like Matt. She started seeing Keith on the side. I should have seen it coming really. Light does attract moths.

Keith was the opposite of Matt. He had long dark hair that hung like a greasy, lifeless, mop at the top of his head. His hobby was playing guitar. I was convinced it was some sort of a front to 'get chicks.' He was that type of guy. He was the opposite of Alana, with no drive for a future. And on that note, I suppose he and I had one thing in common. Our only difference was the fact that he just didn't care. And I did care. A lot.

The upside to Keith was that he was funny but he possessed the type of humor that got annoying and crude after awhile. He was the type of guy to wear dirty clothes 4 times in a row, going purely off the scent lingering in the fabric. I didn't see what Alana saw in him. I thought that maybe she just wanted to stir something up with Matt. But with Keith… there was a reason to be shocked. He was Matt's lazy, going nowhere in life best friend.

So much for best friend, hey?

The only thing Keith had going for him was his girlfriend

Tanya, who was a bitch. But of course she was pretty and popular and outgoing, which was more than I could say for myself. Naturally, she was stunning. She had dark features with olive skin. Her black hair was long and thick like a curtain, her eyes were almond shaped and deep brown. Gorgeous. Which may have explained the tension her and Alana had; that, and the fact that Alana was sleeping with her boyfriend. Even though I didn't know Tanya personally, I didn't like her because my sister didn't. Blindsided as it was, that was reason enough for me.

Alana didn't like a lot of people and in turn, a lot of people tried to impress her. If anyone knew how to play people, it would be her. But she did have her enemies. She was very likable when she was being fake, which she almost always was. It was odd because her best friend was modest and very much the opposite.

Her best friend's name was Angela. Angela had strawberry blond hair cut around her shoulders and paper white skin. She was not the tanning type. If anything she was the one you would gladly hand your sunblock to at the beach because her skin tone was blinding you with its very own band of fluorescent light. Angela was a sweetheart and didn't buy into the drama that my sister created with Tanya. I was surprised that they were friends.

It seemed like everyone had something figured out for themselves to some extent. At the very least, they were all happy. Except for me. I didn't know what I was going to do with my life. At first, I thought the feeling came about because I was just trapped in high school, that maybe a sense of direction would form for me, in one way or another after I graduated. I put so much hope into that idea. And I waited.

But nothing happened for me after I graduated. I was stuck in a small town with no sense of direction and no idea how to get out. Talk about feeling trapped.

One day, in the small town of Golden, where nothing ever seemed to happen, Alana went missing. She left far too many questions in her absence. She had gone to a party and didn't come home. Everything changed that night.

At first, I was confused at Alana's disappearance, as everyone was. But over time, I started to piece together what happened. This is our story.

Ivy - The day everything changed

Stepping out of the shower, I squinted at myself in the mirror. My brown eyes looked lifeless from lack of sleep. Dark bags hung under my dull eyes, exaggerating my exhaustion. A wave of nausea washed over me. Grimacing, I leaned forward over the sink and gulped a mouthful of air. It was the only thing keeping me from vomiting all over the sink.

The beginning of a hangover was the worst. Holding my breath, I started to heave. Gas pushed up my throat and I knew that was a warning. Throwing the toilet seat open, I dry heaved into it. Finally, I vomited acid-like liquid. It was bright yellow. Spitting in disgust, I stood up again only to get a hot flash that radiated through my face, making my skin cold and damp.

Groaning, I scooped up my dirty clothes and whatever I had left of my dignity, before leaving the washroom. The television was on, the droning of the morning news hung in the air. Disinterested, I went straight to my room.

Throwing the door

open, I placed my clothes into the hamper and closed the lid. I shut my door and stumbled towards the blinds, intent on shutting out every ounce of light that was pouring into my room. It wasn't morning for me. I could hardly deal with moving. All I could manage was to crawl into my bed. I had to try hard not to move because I knew if I moved too much it would only result in having to return to the porcelain god and give him my sacrifice. It felt like my death was pending.

Curling into a ball under my covers, I forced myself into a restless sleep with too much tossing and turning.

Eventually, my door was thrown open. It rattled on its hinges and thudded against the wall.

Grunting, I squinted at the light that shone from the light above my head. A boob light. It was such a ridiculous design and it was the only thought I could muster in my dozing state.

"Ivy, where is Alana?" Gran asked.

I managed to move, but hardly. Groaning, I tossed the rest of the blankets off my face.

"There's been a fire, and your sister isn't home."

My blood ran cold at that instant. Tense, I sat up. My mind foggy, I squinted at Gran who stood at the foot of my bed, her forehead knitted in concern. My tension washed away as quickly as it had come, as Gran's words registered.

Rubbing my face, I shot a look at Gran that expressed my annoyance, "I wouldn't be too worried, Gran. You know Alana, she was out partying last night. She's probably just having a rough morning, I'm sure we will see her later," I paused, "Where was the fire, exactly? Tanya's house? Because that would make sense," I laughed. "I bet Alana set her house on fire and is hiding from the cops."

Gran scowled. "This isn't something to joke about, Ivy. And a dry sense of humor like that is unbecoming. The fire was in the woods near *our* house, it was close by."

I squinted at her in shock as she continued.

"The police figure it was kids playing some sort of prank, there was likely alcohol involved. The firefighters were here a couple hours ago. They don't know where it started," Gran shook her head. "Can't imagine kids and how they have fun these days. Why don't they just throw a ball around or talk with their peers, but instead they set fires and find satisfaction in that."

Nodding, I swung my legs over my bed. "I know. It's weird," I looked down at my feet, questioning whether it was time to gather

17

motivation.

"You look awfully tired," Gran said, "Didn't sleep well?"

"I went out last night," I said, my tone more assertive than I intended.

"Oh?" Gran said, her brow furrowed in concern. "Be careful with that, you know how your sister can get a little wild. I would hate for you to start going out partying every weekend." She eyed me up and down, as if that were some sort of an unspoken threat.

"Gran…" I groaned. It wasn't like I was in high school anymore; I didn't need someone to push me to do better. Alana was allowed to do whatever she wanted. But that was also because Alana often fought over her freedom and what she considered fair. It didn't usually match what Gran and grandpa thought was fair.

I, on the other hand, didn't have the energy to fight. I also didn't have seem to have plans. But that's another story.

Gran threw up her hands in defense "Right, not my place." She held her mouth in a tight line, biting her lips together. "I just think it's unproductive, that's all."

"Gran," I said louder, gritting my teeth.

"Okay. I'm done." Gran turned to leave, but managed to scoop up an empty glass that was on my dresser before leaving. I was notorious for not bringing my glasses back into the kitchen. I was grateful her nagging stopped there. Today wasn't a day for anything productive, not even conversation.

After a deep breath, I gathered the strength to walk out of my room and into the hallway. Alana's bedroom door was open. Noting this, I peaked in. It was a mess, as always. Rolling my eyes I walked into the living room. Grandpa was sitting in his chair. He didn't break eyes with the TV to notice my presence.

After a moment of silence he grunted, "Do you know where your sister is? Your grandmother and I are worried sick."

Of course my presence was hardly worth a hello.

Shrugging, I walked into the kitchen. It was all about Alana. If I were to go missing, nobody would notice for at least a couple days. God forbid Alana doesn't come home one night, even though she was twenty. "She's probably fine, I bet she's with friends or something. Or maybe she passed out cold, at the party."

"Well which one is it?" Grandpa asked, his eyes still trained on the television set.

Staring at him in stunned silence, I snapped, "Could be either or both."

Grandpa looked up at me as if suddenly sensing the hostility in my voice. He smiled. "Just kidding."

Forcing a smile that looked more like a wince, I dumped the box of rice krispies over a bowl. I watched them tumble out, one after another and imagined my life as just the same. One day, I was bound to drown. I couldn't help but feel like I was drowning in the expectations that my grandparents held over my head. Maybe it was time to move out. But for that to happen, I had to either get a job or figure out what I wanted to do with my life. Both options seemed dreadful to me.

Sitting down at the table I dug into the rice krispies. The only way I would eat them was if they were layered with sugar. The gritty sugar tasted good after a night of drinking, but swallow after swallow I wondered if I would only end up throwing it back up again. Why I even bothered with eating, I really don't know. Maybe to make it seem like I wasn't drinking as much as I did the night before. Gran was one to take notice to that kind of stuff. I wasn't in the mood to be questioned about last night.

Staring out the window into the woods, I noticed the police were still on site. A couple of officers were staring into the trees, as if looking for something they couldn't quite find. Shocked, I squinted through the glass at the ash covering the ground. The wind

20

was blowing, causing the ash to bound into the air.

Drinking in the sight, I noticed Gran on the back porch lurking towards the trees as I was. She was holding the home phone in her hand. Defeated, she turned and started back in.

"It's not like her to not answer her phone," Gran said, looking down at the phone.

"She'll be home later I'm sure." I shrugged, at a loss of words.

"It doesn't feel right," Gran said, "And with this fire…"

"She will be home later," I repeated.

Robeline – Drama queen

"How do your grandparents treat you?" Robeline asked, her blue pen moving across the pad of paper, her eyes trained on her swirling, rapid writing.

"Fine," I paused, "What does that matter, anyway?"

Robeline sighed, impatient with my question. "It matters more than you may think. Development, especially in the younger stages of your life, is crucial; it helps shape who you are. You did mention that if you were the one to have gone missing, your family wouldn't notice for at least a day? Why would you say that if you didn't believe they treated you differently?"

I rolled my eyes. "Alana was a princess, I really don't think you need me to clarify that."

"So everyone else treated her like a princess?" Robeline asked.

"She wouldn't have it any other way."

Robeline narrowed her eyes.

I leaned forward,

"Imagine the biggest attention whore you know. Times that by twenty and *that* is my sister, Alana."

"You say that like you disrespect that."

I shrugged. "Who doesn't?"

"So I take it, you don't consider yourself anything of that sort," Robeline said, grinning.

My smile vanished.

"With that stunt that you pulled earlier, I'd say you and Alana are more alike that you might know."

I averted my gaze.

I had thrown my tray of food off of the table and screamed as loud as I could. But that was because someone had asked what I had done to be at this place and I didn't have an answer.

Robeline toyed with the blue pen and then started writing as I stared out the window. Sighing, she leaned back, "Okay, let's start with some easier questions. Alana didn't come home, how did that make you feel?"

I couldn't hide my glare, "How do you think it made me feel?" I took a deep breath to try to subside the ache in my chest. That very question lingered in the back of my mind, haunting me. Emotions on the subject had a way of making me even more confused. It was easier to ignore my emotions, even though it had a way of backfiring on me.

"There's no wrong answer," Robeline urged, ignoring my sarcasm. "If you can't access how you felt, you can start by telling me how you acted."

"I guess I never cried over it... Not over the fact that she was gone, anyway."

Robeline tilted her head, as if waiting for more.

"Honestly, I felt relieved... partially. And I know that's a really awful thing to say," I said, cringing after the words left my mouth. I prayed that she wouldn't write that down, it would look so much worse on paper. "It's not like I was relieved she was dead. I didn't know she was dead. I was relieved I could finally go on living my life without feeling pestered... by her presence," I bit my lip. Too much. That explanation was too much. My tooth cut through the skin and my lip started to bleed from the inside. I pressed my lip against my tongue, putting pressure on it and tasting the metallic taste of blood.

Flicking the exposed shoe sole with my left foot, I focused on the sound. It seemed to be hollow in my mind, as if I was the only one who could hear it. My mind wandered in an absent state.

"It's alright," Robeline said, touching my arm. Her dark eyes looked genuine and soft this time and for the first time didn't annoy me. "How were you pestered by her presence?" Robeline asked, "Did she bully you?"

"What? No!" My chest tightened as I crossed my arms. Maybe I wasn't ready yet.

"From your story so far, it seems like Alana had some power over you," Robeline said.

"Alana had power over everyone."

"Particularly, power over you," Robeline corrected me.

"Alana had a belittling personality." I said, averting my gaze. "You couldn't possibly understand because you didn't know Alana," I scoffed, resentment bubbling through me, "She always had to be first, she always had to be better than everyone." I didn't mean to say as much as I already had, but my broken emotions tumbled out as I tried to gather my messy thoughts.

Robeline nodded, scribbling down what I had told her. A thought seemed to pop into her mind and she shrugged, about to ask the simple question, that I had a feeling was coming up. "So Alana didn't want you to be anything like her? Or did you feel too threatened to find yourself in her shadow, even if you did try?"

Grinding my teeth I glared at her, "I could have tried to make something for myself but I would have never beaten her – plain and simple. Even if I were to try, things... would only get worse. All I wanted was to be liked by my sister, and if I were to even try to be her competition, I would regret it. I mean, look at Tanya; Alana destroyed her relationship. That's enough to scare me. Plus, I'm the disgrace of the family, the one who isn't going anywhere in life. I'm number two. I always have been and I always will be," I choked on the last part, the realization of the truth I had just sputtered seemed to hurt me more when I said it aloud.

I shook my head, my frustration growing by the second, "Do you know how that feels? To never be good enough? To never be perfect, when that was all that I wanted?" I stopped and shook my head. "I didn't have the personality to be popular, I wasn't pretty, I wasn't smart, I wasn't clever. I was a shadow. If that." More anger flooded into my chest. It pressed up against my chest, suffocating me and when I released it, it all spewed out.

"I was the ground in the shadow and a nobody. Don't belittle me by asking why I didn't try harder, it doesn't work that way." Release. Taking a deep breath, I recovered but I was still fuming. My heart thudded against my chest and echoed in my ears, my blood pounded against every blood vessel in my body.

Robeline put up her hands in defense. "Ivy, you wouldn't have to beat Alana in some sort of a competition. There wasn't one."

I shook my head. "Well *you* didn't know Alana."

Robeline nodded. "I hope you know there are other things that you could have excelled at, like being smart, generous, loving, even being good at a hobby. I'm sorry about your situation, you must have felt isolated. I know it takes awhile for your values to change after high school. I'm sorry if the question offended you Ivy, that wasn't my intention."

Shaking my head, I fell back into my chair, my anger melting away. "Whatever," I muttered under my breath.

Robeline narrowed her eyes before lowering her pen to her notepad. "Let's move on with your story."

Ivy – A new beginning

It had been awhile since Alana didn't come home. It had been nearly three months. Three months of grieving and trying to put the pieces together. Three months of police and investigators putting their nose where it didn't belong. Three months of constant questioning that dwindled to nothing. Alana's case was a dead end.

However, I couldn't say our family accepted that, or even had a chance to. The pity aimed towards Gran, grandpa and I was nothing short of nauseating. We were known as the broken family that had shattered even more. And although we tried to keep it together as a family, it wasn't easy - not this time around. Most of the time, I found myself locked in my bedroom, cringing at the sobs of frustration that was ongoing in our house. Some days the grief would go away for a bit and give me a sense of temporary relief but it always came back. That was frustrating to say the least. I couldn't see our family ever crawling out of the hole of desperation that we had dug for ourselves. I say that like I belonged there with them. I didn't. I had to refuse my   emotions to stay strong.

I found that avoiding my grandparents was better; it hurt me too much to see them in pain. The only question we all had was whether or not Alana was still alive. For my own piece of mind, I convinced myself she had just moved away and was bad at staying in contact. The mind is a powerful thing; I could usually convince myself if I tried hard enough. It worked fine until the ear splitting, racking sobs from inside our house almost always broke that illusion.

Alana's disappearance was difficult on everyone. But in her absence I almost felt a little better, which was hard for me to accept. Her constant harassing and belittling had taken more of a toll on me than I had previously thought. I didn't have to hide from her or avoid her. She was out of sight and out of mind. It was a relief. That was something I would never say out loud to anyone without someone thinking there was something wrong with me. I was supposed to grieve; I was supposed to cry like everyone else. Despite the expectations, I couldn't seem to grieve properly.

In Alana's absence, I felt it was necessary to finally take a look at my life, and to try to figure out what I wanted to do, but my purpose wasn't surfacing. I was still just as stuck as I was with Alana around, even though life felt lighter... easier.

After a few months everything was close to back to normal.

Although that made me feel awful, considering the fact that people just up and moved on, I knew that that was life and it was better to move on then to be stuck in the past. I missed Alana sometimes. But then again I also knew that she created a lot of havoc. And it was more than her lack of empathy and hurting everyone who she came in contact with.

When I was invited to the 'end of the semester' party with the people who were in college, I thought twice about it. Mostly because I would have to face people who were once in my sister's life and I wasn't sure how I would handle that considering my social anxiety. Also, because I wasn't in college or university and I had no idea what I wanted to do with the rest of my life. I would be out of place.

Maybe it was better than staying holed up in my bedroom all day long, reading books I had already read or surfing the Internet until my eyes were red. It was nice to be invited for once and I felt like if I denied the invitation, I might regret it and not get another chance to see my sister's friends.

Maybe it was juvenile but I had always wanted to spend time with my sister's friends. Obviously social blockades kept me at bay. That, and Alana demanded me to stay away from them. I wasn't even allowed to acknowledge them if they were in the same room as me. Alana would give me a cold glare, her mouth hard pressed in a straight line as if to ask what I was doing. She took social situations way too seriously. She was embarrassed of me, embarrassed to be my sister and embarrassed to even know me.

But it wasn't like it affected me anymore. I had gotten past it to an extent. I really didn't have to deal with it anymore so bygones really were bygones.

Combing my hair out, I stared at my reflection. My hair was a mess and even when I did try to tame the mess that it was, it wasn't working the way I planned. I just wasn't happy with my looks anymore. Not that I ever was. For once it would just be nice to look in the mirror and like myself.

Frustrated, I ran my hairbrush through the tap and then ripped it through my tangled curls. *If it dried that way it might look a little more presentable.* No. Despite the fact that I knew water didn't help with frizz, I was too scared to try hair product. In fact, I would rather walk around as a frizz-ball then to try it because I would look way too different and that was too big of a risk. I was what I was, and it was really too late to change.

Curious, my eyes fell to the shelves below the sink. I could see Alana's makeup bag sticking out in plain view and all I could think about was the possibility of looking decent at a party for the first time. Tension started to grow on me as I continued to contemplate my options. Looking back in the mirror, I noticed my uneven skin tone.

It was enough to make anyone act on impulse.

I pulled out Alana's makeup that was carefully placed on a shelf under the sink when she went missing. Everything of Alana's was put out of sight. It was hard to deal with the emotional turmoil after Alana went missing. The problem was that all of her stuff was still lying around as if she was still very much alive in every inch our house. It was hard to believe that she was really gone.

Half of me still expected to see her come in through the front door, only to be bombarded by questions from Gran and grandpa. I still expected her to come back and inhabit the house the way she used to, lighting up the house with life. I think that was the most difficult part. With the reminders of all of her stuff that was left strewn around it was hard to believe that she wasn't coming home; with each passing day it became more real. That was when Gran put away all of her stuff and closed her bedroom door.

Staring at the bag I remembered the many times it was left

sprawled on the bathroom counter, the contents pouring out. It was in a shimmery makeup bag she had bought after one of her many shopping trips. I didn't ever touch it. I knew Alana would lose it if I did. But now it was in my hands. Contemplating putting it back, I knelt down, placing it back under the sink.

Something stopped me. I was curious. There was no one there to stop me or say I was being an idiot for finally trying this stuff out. So after an internal conflict, I stood back up again, makeup bag in hand. Taking a deep breath, I opened the bag.

It was all makeup I had seen before. Expensive makeup that Alana had left lying around here and there. Although I had already seen what was inside the makeup bag, it all hit me like a punch to the stomach. There were so many memories tied to this stuff. One part of me felt like she was gone for years but another felt like she was still here, lingering in the air, all over our house.

My hand fell upon the cover up. Catching my curious eyes in the mirror, I unscrewed the lid and stared at my reflection. My eyes wandered to the blotchy freckles on my nose. And then to my dark under eye circles I had had for too long since Alana's disappearance. It could only help.

Before I could stop myself, I sponged the light liquid all over my uneven skin tone. Like a blanket, it covered my blotches and under eye circles. My self-esteem seemed to rise a little with every stroke of the sponge, leaving me shocked at the results. I could finally see the magic that makeup was.

It was a relief that Alana and my skin tone were so close. I didn't know how to do my makeup and as embarrassing as that was, I continued with the mascara, figuring it really couldn't be that difficult.

It was that difficult. The second that I touched my eyelashes with the black gunk, I got it all over my eyelid.

Cursing, I ran my hand under water and tried to rub the tar-like, crap off.

At least no one was around to see. Raising the wand, I gave it a second try, shaking hard this time. Carefully, I elongated my eyelashes. Some of my eyelashes clumped together. It was a good thing that my expectations were low.

Despite my first fail in applying makeup, I started to not hate my reflection. I looked significantly better. Now I understood why people used makeup. It was nice to walk around without everyone staring at your flaws.

~

I stood at the Angela's front door and combed my fingers through my hair, self-conscious and deciding whether or not to go inside. It was too late to change my mind anyway; I was already there and I lacked the confidence to even knock on the door. I wondered if that would ever change or if I would eternally be socially awkward. Most times it felt like that was my inevitable fate.

I used to daydream about what it would be like to be able to express myself and be liked. But it was hard to even make a phone call when I was feeling nervous. I was too nervous to speak in fear of stuttering or screw up my speech. It was easier to just shut up and too much effort to be hated for being different.

The door opened and I had an immediate urge to turn and run away as my heart flitted against my ribcage like a frightened bird. Instead, I grit my teeth and forced a smile. I had just arrived and Angela had already noticed me; there was no way I could run now. "Hey Angela," I said, smiling a little too wide to conceal my discomfort. I wondered if she could see the dread that was leaking through my false excitement.

The music inside her town house pounded, as my heart continued to thud against my rib cage. Gridding my teeth, I looked past her into the house.

Much to my surprise, Angela didn't seem to notice my nerves, "Hey Ivy, how are you doing?" She stepped aside and let me walk in. Tense, I stumbled in and started to take off my shoes. "Are you wearing makeup?" Angela asked.

Barking a laugh, I nodded. "Yeah, actually."

"Looks good," Angela said raising her eyebrows, "You look good."

Smiling, I nodded. I didn't know what to say. Why did I suck at something as simple as communicating? Wincing, I looked down. Angela looked good too, she always did. Her blonde hair was cut into a bob and she could pull it off well. She wore a lot of shimmery eye shadow that made her small eyes pop out on her delicate face.

"Come on in," Angela said. Matt came from around the corner at that second.

"Oh, there you are," Matt smiled, noticing Angela immediately. I averted my gaze, avoiding confrontation with my sister's boyfriend. Shockingly, it was even more awkward now that Alana was gone. Every time I saw him all I could think about was Alana. I didn't want to think about Alana.

"Oh, hey Ivy," Matt said noticing me a second after. He

stared at me a little longer, letting the silence set in.

"Come on," Angela grabbed Matt's arm and wheeled him around.

Following behind them, I looked blankly ahead as they continued their conversation. I was out of place, yet relieved that at least I could drink soon to ease my nerves. I had to turn to something to keep me normal.

I had graduated from twisted teas to harder drinks, like vodka. It also hit my head faster and the light feeling was what I needed to gently ease myself into this situation.

Collapsing onto a bare love seat, I mixed myself a drink in front of Angela, Matt, Keith and, of course Tanya who were all sitting on the couches around me. They seemed to watch me, full of curiosity and mild judgment. After all, I was supposed to display the signs of a forever-mourning sister.

They stared at me like they were waiting for me to explode and collapse into tears about my sister. I really didn't know what they expected but they stared just the same, waiting for something. Maybe they expected a grand gesture but I didn't have one. A lot of awkward situations that were presented in my life were more inside my head but I was acutely aware of the situation in front of me. It made me want to turn around and leave. It was too late for that, and if I left now it would be socially unacceptable.

I didn't know any of Angela's other friends that were swarming through the house. Oddly enough, the fact that there were people I didn't know seemed to ease my nerves. Focusing on them, I hoped the attention would come off of me. I raised my drink to my lips and Matt interrupted,

"Vodka slime?" He cleared his throat.

"Yeah, they're not bad, I guess I'm falling into Alana's footsteps," I paused, regretting saying it after her name rolled off my tongue. Instantly my face flushed with heat. It had been too long and I was getting over not saying her name. But just because I was over it didn't mean that everyone else was too. I was more aware of that as the seconds passed, feeling like full minutes with exchanging glances and confused looks. I had made the situation uncomfortable for everyone, especially myself. Just like I imagined I would.

Although I thought about Alana's whereabouts and if she was still alive, it was something that most people weren't able to cope with and especially not with others. Which was understandable. How wrong was it to question the situation and reach for a larger truth? Everyone else seemed to cower away from knowing what happened. They all tried to live as though she wasn't even a thought. I made the mistake of convincing myself that she was gone on a very long vacation. It would have helped if I thought more like them.

It wasn't my fault I thought differently. I should have been able to bring her up casually without getting looks of disapproval. Dwelling on what was gone seemed pointless. Alana wasn't coming back so choking on her name didn't seem worth it. She was a huge part of our lives at one time. Granted her situation was beyond devastating. And, well, I was an awkward person and for some reason I always said the wrong things. My thoughts had a way of sounding stupid out loud. I guess that's a nice way to put it.

The room grew quiet. I noticed I had made everyone within earshot uncomfortable. I swallowed the growing apple in my throat. "Sorry," I blurted.

Tanya shrugged, "Oh well, moving on," she grabbed Keith's hand and he looked away, embarrassed. Most people knew about him and Alana now. It was exploited after Alana went missing.

Keith and Matt were the biggest suspects. Matt was a suspect because he confronted Alana with the big issue of their relationship the night she went missing. He wouldn't do anything to hurt Alana. If the police had known that they were fighting that night he would be wrongly convicted.

I glanced over at Matt who was sitting beside Angela. He looked around the room as if he wished he were anywhere but there. The talk of his dead girlfriend seemed to make him uneasy. I couldn't blame him. I felt sorry for him.

Matt caught my stare and shifted his gaze, a troubled look crossing his light eyes. He tore his gaze away from me and grasped Angela's pale hand. I couldn't help but stare.

"So is there anyone else coming?" Matt asked Angela. His tone fell flat, expressing the haste in his change of conversation.

"I told everyone to show up around 10, but of course the later it gets, the more people show up," Angela responded lightly, her eyes lingering on Matt.

Glancing down at my drink, I let uncomfortable silence set in. It was at that moment I really wished I would have stayed home.

"So you guys are together, I'm assuming?" Tanya more or less, announced. It was just like her to make everybody else even more embarrassed. Grinning, she brushed her dark hair over her shoulder like a veil and leaned forward. "You two would make a really cute couple." Keith shot Tanya a look of shock.

Heat rose from my stomach up my throat. I shot a glare

towards Tanya. I could completely understand why my sister hated her. Angry, I glanced at Matt, waiting for his response, knowing whatever he was about to say would anger me even more. I could see the truth all over him already.

It was too soon. Was I the only person that thought that?

The light skin on Angela's pale cheeks flushed deep red. She looked up at Matt and impossibly, her blush deepened.

I took a gulp of alcohol, letting it slide down my throat. I was waiting. Waiting for them to admit they were in love and about to elope, maybe they were going to adopt a puppy like every other newly in love couple. That was ridiculous, I knew that, but I couldn't help but expect to hear it from the way he was looking at her. It had been years since he looked at Alana like that. Alana... My missing sister.

"Isn't it a little soon?" I asked. *And* I spoke when I should have left it as a thought. My face flushed. Part of me didn't think anyone would hear it, the other part of me wanted to yell it. Ah, the effects of alcohol. "I mean it's only been a few months," I reasoned, picking myself back up, my face burning hotter as everyone turned to me.

The looks of pity that I got at that moment were almost

sickening. "I'm sorry, I guess this hits me harder than anyone, and I mean, you were her best friend," I said, nodding to Angela, hoping she would pick up what I was trying so hard not to yell. I realized it wouldn't sink in when Angela's innocent blue eyes widened. She was too naïve to understand what I was trying to get at. Didn't she see that this was morally...wrong? Or at least weird.

Although I was aware I was embarrassing myself, I also couldn't seem to help it. "I just wonder what she would think of this that's all." I took a sip of my drink. When I looked up, I caught every eye in the room trained on me, waiting for an even bigger explosion. It made me realize my head was light with the amount of alcohol I had downed.

Gritting my teeth, I felt their eyes burning into me. It was best to just stop. My anger was taking control now and it wasn't working out for my benefit, I couldn't help but feel a bubble of anger growing so large inside me. Instead of having people reason with what I was saying, I was getting more looks of confusion. How cruel it was of me to ask so much of Matt than to at least take respect in the fact that his girlfriend was missing. Or ex - whatever she would be. What I was saying didn't even make sense to them. "Sorry," I muttered.

Angela opened her mouth in shock.

Tanya spat out a laugh and leaned back into Keith's arms, her face lit up in amusement. Her laughter set me off. I tried to mute my anger.

"It's just… I can't even mention her name and here you guys are, dating or whatever. I just think it's weird." I said, looking around the room, half hoping for someone - anyone in the room to agree with me. Why wasn't I just shutting up?

Keith leaned forward, "I think that we should all just move on and try to go on living our lives like this didn't happen. We would all be better off." Everyone in earshot nodded.

I shot him a look of suspicion. "What do you mean?" I was on a roll tonight.

Keith looked around the room and then at Tanya. She nodded. "I just think we should all move on and try to go on living our lives because it's just not working putting so much…" he paused, "Grief into this."

"After two and a half months," I said. "We can't grieve for longer than two and a half months?" Sarcasm dripped from my tone. It was closer to three but I was trying my best to make it sound worse than it was. It wasn't like Alana's friends would carefully count back the days to make sure I was accurate, besides, stretching the truth is a good way to improve my argument. My blurred conscience would agree, anyway.

"If he wants to date her, how is that any of your business?" Tanya asked, leaning forward, a smug look on her face. "Alana was a bitch anyway," She paused and looked around for approval. I think even she knew it was wrong to speak ill of the dead. Or missing. I wish she had a filter. At that moment, I felt rage seeping into my throat. I held back and took a deep breath, falling back into the love seat in defeat. There was no winning with these people; they would all believe Keith's childish idea of 'we should all move on because it was easier than grieving.' I suppose that was the norm.

Taking a sip of my vodka slime, I watched the way Matt placed his hand on Angela's back and the way he smiled at her when she looked up at him. Maybe he really cared about her. Either way, it still didn't make it right.

Alana - Back to the party - (three months ago)

"Alana... You're here," Tanya said, her voice falling flat. She held the door open but refused to step aside, her brown eyes wide. She smiled a fake smile that looked wiry and awkward on her red, painted lips. I knew she didn't like me but she could try a littler harder to pretend. It was clear she had a bit too much to drink, which made her stumble in the doorway.

"Of course I am!" I grinned and cocked my head to the side. "Tanya – it's 9:00PM, and you're already drunk?"

"I'm not drunk," Tanya slurred, stumbling back. "And I'm pretty sure *you* weren't invited,"

"Pretty sure nobody cares," I flashed a smile.

Tanya scowled and re-gained her balance. The people by the doorway started to stare, as if waiting for a full-on brawl to go down. If Tanya were smart, she wouldn't have confronted me. Then again, she was drunk and stupid and the two just don't mix.

"Maybe you should take it easy on the booze," I said, clapping Tanya on the back.

Stepping past her, I surveyed the area for familiar faces.

"Alana! Come here," Matt called out. Shutting him out, I strolled into the house, on an aimless mission.

"Alana, you came!" I heard Angela, my best friend calling across the room. She was sitting on a stool talking to Keith. Her blue eyes widened in surprise.

"Why is everyone so shocked I'm here?" I asked looking around the room at all the familiar faces. Then I shot a look at Tanya. Oh right, how could I forget? Too bad nobody cared about invites anymore. In fact it was kind of badass that I was technically 'crashing' her little party.

Music pounded through the house, making it difficult to hear anyone. Still, there was a buzz in the air, excitement. The weekend was finally here. I was more than relieved about that. My course load was becoming a little much for me. Still, it was like my past was following me around.

I recognized most of the people in the house. Recognized but that doesn't mean spoke to. I would have rather put my face through a wall than converse with some of the people I went to high school with. I averted my gaze from the annoying clan of girls that would get disgustingly obliterated and tell me about how they thought I "hated" them in high school.

I didn't know them. Somehow, that was even more offensive to them.

So I would have to explain that no, I, in fact, do not hate them and I have chronic bitch-face and I didn't know them, (and I didn't care to know them) blah blah blah. I wasn't in the mood for that.

Plus, I've learned that I tend to tell the truth after a drink or two. Me + alcohol + small talk really doesn't work. Because then I start to tell the truth and it turns out a lot of people can't handle my opinion. Which in a lot of cases they could benefit from. I guess that's what you get for giving constructive criticism.

Then again, I also get cocky and self absorbed while drinking. I felt all around better.

Technically speaking, alcohol doesn't make anyone better, except for me of course because I was hilarious while drunk. The buzz is what helps us forget our lives temporarily and there's nothing better then escaping sometimes. Everything is better in a sense. In saying that, alcohol tears down those social blockades people try so hard to keep up. Then things get fun. Things they don't want exploited suddenly become the topic of the night. Some go home with people they've hardly talked to-or worse, someone they're close to. Alcohol creates that stumbling, blubbering mess that falls into everything and cries at an issue blown way out of proportion. But if you handle it right, it could create a pretty wicked night.

However, most people couldn't control themselves or know their limits. Which is hilarious to watch, not so hilarious to deal with.

Keith was sitting with Matt on the couch. That should have been warning enough. However, I was willing to stir something up for a more interesting night. Why not?

Collapsing on the couch across from the two, I exchanged meaningful glances toward Keith, Tanya's boyfriend. His eyes darted away as if scared his best friend would catch the look I was giving him. Or worst yet, his girlfriend. Making someone uncomfortable just by a look. I guess that could be taken two ways. But I took it as a compliment because I may as well. I noticed the blood rush up Keith's neck to his cheeks. I couldn't help but smile with satisfaction.

Grabbing the bottle of vodka on the table, I mixed a strong cup of vodka slime in a red party cup that was likely Matt's. It was empty, therefore, clean enough. I forced down a swig, cringing at the bitter taste of it, but enjoying the immediate, hot sensation in the pit of my stomach. The taste of vodka was nauseating at the same time. It reminded me of the last time I vomited up the stuff. It would take a couple drinks before they went down smooth. That, or I had to give up the drink entirely. Similar to my experience with red wine.

The first time I got drunk on red wine was at Christmas. I was fourteen and it was just the four of us that year. Gran would claim to actually love the taste of red wine. She went so far to say it was a delicate fruity taste. Why did I only taste gasoline? It was a struggle to not gag on the brawny aftertaste.

Of course, Ivy was too much of an anxiety-ridden kid to finish her glass ,while I stole a few more after the first. Every now and again, Gran and grandpa would indulge in wine and it was my opportunity to do it with them and the more they drank the more they seemed to not notice how much I was stealing. I wasn't an innocent kid. I wanted to know what it was like to get "wasted." Nonetheless, I could never understand casual drinking. When I drank - I had only one goal in mind. There was no pleasure in sipping poison.

Lifting the drink to my lips again, I forced a swig down, the memory still lingering in my thoughts. I didn't notice that I had downed my drink while thinking so hard.

When I looked up, I caught Matt and Keith staring at me. I

laughed and set the empty cup down on the coffee table. "Just a drink to get the night started," I assured them. An absent look crossed Keith's face as he looked down at my glass on the table. Cocking my head to the side, I flashed a smile at him but he refused to acknowledge it. Instead, he jumped up and walked towards the washroom.

"Well then." I blinked in shock, a pang of anger coursed through me. He was probably looking for Tanya. The thought made me feel physically ill. I hated how he still tried to make things work with her. As if it hadn't already hit the end of that relationship. Yet he was impulsive enough to have me when he wanted me.

I was pissed at how he left me to find Tanya. There was no reason for him to continue to coddle her. Why the hell didn't he feel that way about me yet?

In the end, I was the one that was going to look like the idiot - and that wasn't okay with me. That wasn't how this was supposed to end. My tiny crush on Keith had snowballed into something that made me feel completely and utterly stupid. I was ashamed that I gave him power over my feelings. That, and the fact that I was still dating Matt. I lifted the drink to my lips and downed the rest of it.

I caught Matt staring at me, his eyes dark. He was thinking

but unable to say anything to me. Shifting my eyes from his, I stood up and started towards the washroom.

From the corner of my eye, I saw Ivy's face, standing out of the crowd like a fucking sore thumb. The mere sight of her made me sick, she was poorly dressed, as usual. Her frizzy hair looked even more fried. When she caught sight of me the blood drained out of her face. She started towards me.

My jaw clenching, I tried to hold my anger in as Ivy approached me. "What do you think you're doing here?" I demanded.

Ivy blinked with shock at my tone. "Well I just didn't want to sit at home alone again and I thought it would be no big deal..."

"You thought wrong," I snapped. "This is embarrassing. *You* are embarrassing."

Ivy shook her head. "Stop. It isn't a big deal."

"Isn't a big deal?" I laughed and then noticed a couple people were staring. I yanked Ivy by the arm into the washroom and shut the door, careful to press the lock. Taking a deep breath, I gathered my thoughts, "Let's get something straight. It's believable that I was invited to this because I'm *actually* friends with all of these people, you," I coughed a laugh, "No way. So you are unnecessarily embarrassing me as well as yourself. So leave."

Tears began to sparkle in Ivy's eyes. "I just wanted to ask you what's wrong."

I shook my head, "None of your god damn business, Ivy, my life doesn't involve you."

Tears spilled over the edges of Ivy's brown eyes. "It feels like you just hate me no matter what I do."

"How could I not hate you?" I demanded. "I mean, even right now you're acting like an emotional twelve year old, get over yourself, you're not in high school anymore. You can't be pulling shit like this anymore. What were you thinking showing up to a party where you don't know anyone?"

Ivy's face turned red. "I know Matt and Angela and Tanya sort of."

"How do you know Tanya?" I demanded.

"I ran into her when I first walked in," Ivy said.

"Oh god," I muttered. I turned around and checked myself over in the mirror. My lipstick needed to be retouched. Pulling out the tube from my purse, I lined my bottom lip carefully. "Just because you talk to someone once, Ivy, doesn't mean you know them. And for gods sake don't talk to *that* bitch."

Ivy's tears seemed to vanish as she watched me apply my

makeup in the mirror, focused on the movement of the lipstick. "Funny, she said the same thing about you," Ivy said.

Slicking the lipstick over my lips, I took a step back to admire the finish. "Is that so?" I muttered.

"Yeah she told me you're screwing her boyfriend," Ivy said, her tone flat.

I caught her eyes in the mirror but averted my eyes to pull on my clothes and readjust. I had to look hot.

"Is it true?" Ivy asked.

I spun around and leaned back on the counter. "Are you ever going to stop meddling in my life? Or are you destined to be a fucking loser?" I cringed at the ice in my tone. It was so easy to get frustrated with her. I sighed, "You have got to stop associating with me. My life is none of your business."

Ivy raised her eyebrows. "Tell me if it's true."

"Maybe." A grin grew over my face as I continued to adjust myself in the mirror.

"It is, isn't it?" Ivy asked. Her face paled in the side of the mirror.

Letting out a sigh, I crossed my arms in front of me. "There's a chance that I *accidentally*... began to get feelings for Keith."

Ivy stepped back, her face red. "I knew it," she muttered. "I knew you would do this. It's not fair Alana, break up with Matt."

"So you think you have a say in this?" I asked, barking a laugh. "Get out of here. And once you leave this bathroom don't stop walking until you get home. You don't know these people, they're *my* friends, not yours."

Ivy's face turned to stone. Emotionless.

One of two things would happen, she would either choke on her words or lose her breath. I called it "choking." It was one of the weird things that my sister would do - as if breathing was really that difficult. Her face was priceless. *Just breathe, you idiot.*

Instead of her usual loss of breath, Ivy spun around on her heel and stormed out the door. I flinched as she slammed the door behind her.

Rolling my eyes, I turned my attention back to the mirror. I forced a smile and threw my hair over my shoulder. Beaming with confidence, I burst through the door back out into the party. I scanned the room for a familiar face. Matt's eyes caught mine from across the room. He didn't look happy.

I scanned the room for Ivy. I was ready to tear out her throat. But I couldn't find her in 0.03 seconds so I started to walk briskly towards Angela. "Mind if I steal a drink?" I asked, dunking my hand in her box of coolers and answering the question for her.

Angela looked up at me, "Uh, sure." Her eyes focused behind me and a tremor rolled up my spine.

Matt's voice made me jump. "We have to talk," he said. He noticed the drink in my hand and pried it out of my reach before I could open it. "Don't want you to drink too much and do something stupid," he reasoned, I could hear him smiling through his voice, as if it was completely normal for him to make my choices for me. He did have a way of putting on a show in front of other people. Angela wouldn't notice, partially because she was oblivious, partially because she was stupid. I knew better.

Matt placed his other hand behind my neck, under my hair, his forefinger and thumb pressed into the back of my neck like he was ready to throw me into a wall. "You do seem to do a lot of stupid things when you're drinking," Matt said, his tone half-playful.

"I was j-just talking with Angela." Did I just stutter? Swallowing heavily, I looked back at him wide-eyed.

Matt's blue eyes were cold. "Oh? I'm sure it can wait."

My breath caught in my throat. I exchanged a look of panic around the room, anything to get my attention away from the current situation. Angela's eyes widened at my reaction to Matt, as if I was the one who was acting up.

Barking a laugh I looked up at him. "Uh okay?" My voice was snarky but I started to shake. The fact this moment was coming wasn't such a shock to me, although I just didn't expect it so soon. Smashing back to reality, I turned around on rubber legs, my head fuzzy with a slight buzz.

We went to the kitchen, Matt seeming to drag me by my upper arm. Of course, he was beside me, so it didn't look out of character to anyone around us. That's something that we were both good at - keeping up appearances.

Inconvenient enough, the alcohol just hit me and it was getting harder to walk straight. We walked outside. The fresh air seemed to sober me up a bit but not near enough for the conversation we were about to have.

Matt started pacing in front of me as I stood against the fence, at a loss of what to say or do or say. Finally Matt spoke, his voice shaking. "I don't understand. If you didn't want to be with me why couldn't you just break up with me? Instead you make this mess. You made me hate my best friend. How messed up is that?"

I opened my mouth to answer and then realized there was no

way I was talking my way out of this. There was no way anything intelligent would come out of me at that moment anyway, so it was probably best to just shut up. Instead of listening to what he was saying, I focused on the sounds of the quiet night and the fresh air, hoping for the conversation to end or for him to end it with me or *something*.

"Matt, we're in college," I said finally, shrugging. I didn't know what I meant or maybe I was just trying to hide it form myself. It was the best I could come up with. Wincing, I waited for Matt to blow up at my observation that was clearly leading nowhere he would like.

Matt looked taken aback and at a loss for words. He shrugged finally as a look of understanding crossed his face, "Then why date? If you just want to fuck around why would you pretend you were still in this relationship? Did you do it to wreck my relationship with my best friend? Why did you do this?"

I looked around. "For entertainment I guess..." I braced, waiting for the angry response. That was stupid. That was really stupid. I didn't even know why I was doing this. It was getting harder to be with him. It just wasn't worth it anymore. Why was it so hard to just say that?

"Fuck Alana, really?" He yelled suddenly. "Really?!" He then took a running kick at the nearest plastic chair. "This is bullshit!" He bellowed. I watched in silence as the chair slammed against the wooden fence.

I'd seen this side of him before. It made me sober up in an instant. The crowd screamed with excitement in the house. I stayed paralyzed against the side of the house, wishing we weren't alone. How parallel I felt while being pressed against the side of the house, as everyone inside was having the time of their lives. In that moment, I felt like I had turned to stone. I could hear my breathing getting louder and more rapid.

The sad part is, some part of me really didn't want to let him go. The other part of me was laughing at his anger and pushing me to provoke him further.

Ivy – Back to the party - (three months ago)

I had followed Alana to the party. It wasn't my scene but I was tired of sitting at home alone. So I snuck in through the back door of Tanya's house. I couldn't seem to control myself anymore; I was just so tired of not doing anything with my life. I was tired of not having friends and not even bothering to socialize because I was Alana's weird little sister.

So when the opportunity presented itself, I took it, not bothering to think it through. If I thought too much about it, I would change my mind. You could blame it on the apparent midlife crisis I was having at the ripe old age of 19.

Nobody would think anything of it, there were so many people crammed into Tanya's house; people would think my sister brought me along… Even though that was unrealistic and Alana would kill me if she knew I was there. Only a select few would know that. It was safe enough.

I was cautious as I opened the door and peaked in. A guy in the corner scowled at me because I was still peeking through the door like an idiot, too scared to make a move.

But then I remembered my frizzy, curly, dull hair; it was enough to make anyone stare. Either he was staring at me because of my awful hair or maybe it was my lack of makeup that wasn't doing me any favors. I walked inside and flashed an awkward grin at the guy who gave me a dirty look. He looked away.

It was then that I ran into Tanya on her way to the washroom. She was drunk and muttering to herself as she stumbled towards me as if on a mission. Scowling she looked me over in surprise. "Who invited you?" she slurred, sloshing her drink into the air and regretfully a bit on her leopard shirt. She didn't seem to notice.

"I came with my sister," I lied, averting my eyes from her cold glare. I hoped she wouldn't pursue the question further because my heart was racing at the idea of Alana knowing I was there. My goal was to dodge her all night.

I looked past Tanya at Alana. She was sauntering towards Matt and Keith who were sitting on the couch. She was wearing black stiletto's that seemed a little overdone for a party. Her tight blue skirt and black tank top seemed even more overdone. Then again, what did I know considering my naked face, frizzy hair and over-sized hoodie? Everything about Alana was overdone. Everything about me was tragically underdone.

"Fuck that you did," Tanya laughed, seeing through my lie. "We all know your sister hates you," she informed me, slicing through every ounce of security I had.

A rush of sadness rushed through every nerve ending in my body. I knew Alana hated me. But being *told* that she hated me seemed to make it real. I wondered if it was common knowledge. I thought my sister had the decency to at least keep her hatred for me between her and I. With an ache in my throat, I avoided Tanya's unsympathetic glare.

Tanya shot a look toward Keith who was checking out Alana. "She thinks I don't know she's sleeping with my boyfriend. Of course I know," Tanya turned to me. "It's embarrassing. Everyone knows," she said, tears forming in her brown eyes. She wiped them away with frustration. "At least you're not a little bitch like your sister."

I glanced around the room in panic. Alana was cheating on Matt... With Keith?! I looked toward Alana who was tossing back drinks while sitting with Matt and Keith. How could he not know?

"Sometimes I'm not sure Alana knows that her actions affect others," I said in attempt to get more information out of Tanya.

"Oh, she knows damn well," Tanya corrected me, "she just hates me because I'm competition and she's not used to it. She should just die," she snapped her dark eyes lighting up with her outburst of anger.

I cocked my head to the side, "Excuse me?" I didn't give her a second to respond. "Don't threaten my sisters life over a guy," I snapped in Alana's immediate defense. My face flushed in anger, my ears hot.

Tanya shot me a look. "Fix you're fucking hair," she said before pushing past me and into the washroom. She didn't bother to close the door. Instead she heaved on the toilet, her back arching with every dry heave. Turning my head in disgust, I waited for the sickening sound of vomit. It gushed into the toilet, echoing from the washroom. Nice. Scowling, I turned away.

Although Tanya's comment hit hard, it was something that didn't affect me as much as I thought it would. In her defense, I really did have to fix my fucking hair.

When I looked up, all I saw was Alana's face crushed with the look of indecision. Keith wasn't sitting with her anymore either.

Suddenly, Alana lifted her eyes to mine, her expression soft with confusion. Then her face twisted with anger. My heart raced in my chest with the realization that I had been caught. But she looked upset so it was possible that if I consoled her she would let me stay. I walked towards her, uncertain of my own motives.

"What do you think you're doing here?" Alana demanded, her blue eyes flaring with hatred at the sight of me. She looked me over, scrutinizing every detail of what I was wearing.

"Well I just didn't want to sit at home alone again and I thought it would be no big deal..." I said. My lungs started to constrict.

"You thought wrong," Alana snapped. "This is embarrassing. *You* are embarrassing."

I shook my head, "Stop. It isn't a big deal." The feeling of disappointment made my chest constrict. It was a familiar feeling.

"Isn't a big deal?" Alana scoffed loudly and then looked around the room; careful to make sure no one was over hearing our conversation. She grasped my arm in a firm grasp and pulled me to the washroom that was a few feet away. Pushing me inside, she slammed the door behind us and turned to me. "Lets get something straight. It's believable that I was invited to this because

I'm *actually* friends with all of these people, you," she snorted, "No way. So you are unnecessarily embarrassing me, as well as yourself. So leave."

I blinked in shock at her harsh tone, in turn, my breathing became shallow. "I just wanted to ask you what's wrong."

"None of your god damn business, Ivy, my life doesn't involve you," Alana snapped.

It was as if Alana had plunged a knife into my stomach. Like she was finalizing the fact that she wanted nothing to do with me whatsoever and all I ever wanted was to be her sister. She didn't want anything to do with me. Tears started to leak from my eyes before I could change my train of thought to avoid it. "It feels like you just hate me no matter what I do," I blurted, the complete feeling of drowning filling my chest. I couldn't breathe. It was getting harder to breathe around her.

"How could I not hate you?" Alana snapped, "I mean, even right now you're acting like an emotional twelve year old, get over yourself, you're not in high school anymore. And what were you thinking showing up to a party where you don't know anyone?"

My face went hot out of embarrassment. "I know Matt and Angela and Tanya sort of."

"How do you know Tanya?" Alana demanded, her eyes widening.

"I ran into her when I first walked in," I said.

"Oh god," Alana said, as if embarrassed by my response, she spun around and looked herself over in the mirror. Her eyes stared at her own lips in the mirror and she dove into her purse to retrieve a tube of lipstick. She lined the deep red color along her bottom lip with steady precision.

Alana caught my stare in the mirror and continued, "Just because you talk to someone once, Ivy, doesn't mean you know them. And for gods sake don't talk to that bitch."

It was a wonder why I was talking to the bitch in front of me. I thought back to the conversation I had with Tanya. "Funny, she said the same thing about you," I said.

Alana leaned back to admire herself "Is that so?" she muttered, disinterested as she mashed her lips together, blending the dark lipstick.

"Yeah, she told me you're screwing her boyfriend," I said.

Alana glanced at me in the mirror for only a second, she continued to readjust her clothes, twisting in the mirror to catch all angles of her outfit.

"Is it true?" I demanded, my heart thudding against my chest.

Alana spun around and leaned back onto the counter, "Are you ever going to stop meddling in my life? Or are you destined to be a fucking loser? You have got to stop associating with me. My life is none of your business."

Forcing a deep breath, I pushed the insults out of my head. My voice shaking, I persisted. "Tell me if it's true."

"Maybe," Alana smiled, her cheeks flushing faint on her pale skin. She glanced at my expression in the mirror.

"It is, isn't it?" I answered the question for her. I couldn't breathe again.

Alana sighed and crossed her arms, "There's a chance that I began to get feelings for Keith."

"I knew it," I accused. "I knew you would do this. It's not fair Alana, break up with Matt." My face flushed in anger. This was typical of Alana. She only cared about herself.

Alana barked a laugh. "That's hilarious. Do you actually think you have a say in *my* life?" She laughed again. "Get out of here. And once you leave this bathroom don't stop walking until you get home. You don't know these people, they're *my* friends, not yours."

An uncontrollable anger surged through me, lighting my nerve endings with fire. My lungs were officially full of water, like the beginning of a panic attack. I forced a rattled breath. I wasn't going to let Alana get away with it this time. I stormed out of the bathroom and slammed the door. I couldn't control myself. Scanning the crowd, I found Matt.

Alana was done screwing Matt over. In a blind rage, I found myself in front of Matt in a couple seconds flat.

"I hope you know your girlfriend is screwing your best friend," I told him, my face burning hotter with every word. I took a deep breath after the words exploded out of my mouth.

Matt's eyes widened in shock.

I opened my mouth to say more but it was like I had just woken up from a dream; my anger was unaware of the consequences of my actions. *Whoops*. I choked on everything I wanted to say and turned to run away from my accident.

I ran towards the back door that I had come in through earlier. Stopping in front of the door, I turned around, indecisive on whether I should listen to my sister and go home.

It would be satisfying to see the look on Alana's face when

Matt broke up with her. I had to stay around for that at least.

I spun back around and pressed my back against the wall. I struggled to catch my breath, my face still hot. Flustered, I looked into my over-sized bag that I had since high school. It used to carry all of my books in school. It was tie-dyed and beaten up and now it was crammed full of twisted teas. Taking one out, I struggled with the "twist top" that cut into my hands. I wasn't an experienced drinker.

"Need help with that?" Keith asked, showing up at my side. I leaped into the air, shocked that someone had noticed me when I felt so invisible.

I wanted to say no or to leave but instead, I stayed planted on to the ground, forced by my need to be polite. The idea that Keith was standing right beside me itched at me because it would be just a matter of time before Alana noticed me with Keith by my side. I turned to face him head on, my back to the room so Alana wouldn't be able to see my face if she looked my way.

I looked up at Keith's superman shirt and I stared at it. Keith twisted the top off my drink and passed it back to me. Noticing that I was staring at his shirt, he bobbed his head up and down as if to nod slowly, "you like?"

I couldn't tell whether Keith meant him or the shirt. With him, you never knew, but I was going with shirt. "Um," I paused and took a big swig of my drink. "It's alright."

"Just alright?" Keith asked, his dark eyes dancing like I had told a joke. "It's awesome, okay?"

"Okay," I said, already finding his presence irritating. His attempt at conversation was even more irritating. But it got my mind off of what I had just done, so I stayed glued to the floor. "It's alright," I repeated, taking a huge swig of my drink, and examining the room.

"You remind me of your sister," Keith laughed.

"Really?" I asked, turning back to him.

"I mean about the way you drink," Keith said, grinning. "Be careful or you'll be loaded pretty quick."

I looked away in embarrassment that I thought he meant something else. That maybe I reminded him of my sister because there was something about me that was attractive or special or different.

Downing the whole bottle, I nodded at Keith's comment. Little did he know that getting 'loaded' was my exact intention.

Suddenly weary of Keith's presence, I looked him over. I

couldn't understand why my sister would risk her relationship with Matt to be with such a… greaser like Keith. She could do better. She was doing better. Then again, there were a lot of things about Alana that didn't make sense. If I were in her position and lucked out with life, I would have appreciated it, unlike her. Unfortunately, life doesn't work that way. Who knows, maybe with the wrong type of attention, I wouldn't have appreciated it either.

I popped off the lid of the second twisted tea, not so much noticing the pain of the lid cutting into my palm; the alcohol numbed me. I was buzzing to say the least.

"So how's my sister," I asked Keith, breaking the silence. I noticed that I was actually wanting to talk to Keith about Alana after downing my first drink. It was beginning to hit me, and hard. Normally, I would be embarrassed to ask a question that would make all of the blood drain out of Keith's face but tonight I didn't care. It was entertainment and my mind was fogging over, which made questions like that more appropriate. Grinning, I took another large sip of my drink.

Just like I thought he would, Keith looked around, incredulous by what he thought was me ratting him out.

"You are close with her right?" I asked, smirking. My face

started to burn. I knew I would regret this when I was sober, yet the fact that I didn't like Keith seemed to make it okay.

Keith stood in stunned silence. Then he looked past me into the bathroom where Tanya was bent over the toilet, and once again, with the door wide open as if she ran in just in time. "What's your problem?" he asked, his eyes flashing in anger.

I shrugged, "Am I making you uncomfortable?" After all, it was just a question.

He squinted his dark eyes at me. "What kind of game are you playing? You know your sister made a choice."

"So did you." I looked past him toward Tanya, still in the washroom but now draped over the toilet like a used hand towel.

"I don't think you understand," Keith said, "I still love Tanya but Alana…" He paused as if he couldn't see where he was going with his explanation. Neither could I.

Feeling light on my feet, I shifted my weight and downed a bit more of my drink, intent on keeping my buzz. It was at that point that I realized I was getting drunk fast. Which explained my comebacks. "But Alana…" I continued on for him, waiting for a reason. "Alana's hot? Or you're selfish?" I blinked at shock as the words slipped out.

"Just do yourself a favor and fuck off," Keith growled, pushing past me toward Tanya.

Enjoying the drama, I lifted my drink to him in cheers and let out a giggle. Then I caught sight of Alana turning around, Matt's hand on her upper arm. She was wobbly on her high heels, her face blank. Panicking, I turned around and peered out the window into the back yard. If anything, Alana catching sight of me was the worst-case scenario. She knew for sure I told Matt and she was unpredictable; I didn't know whether she would embarrass me in front of everyone or just yell at me when we were at home. Either way, it was worth avoiding.

The door slammed beside me and I jumped up in shock. Relief sunk through me. Downing the rest of my drink, I tossed the bottle into my bag where it clanged against the other bottles crammed in my bag. I was now sporting a strong buzz and it felt good to not care.

Out of curiosity, I looked out the window. Alana stood against the fence, timid. I had never seen her look so ashamed as she did in that moment. She almost looked child-like, helpless. Matt paced in front of her, his anger making his light blue eyes darken. Alana started to talk, shrugging a lot and looking down in shame almost immediately as Matt yelled at her. He then threw a lawn chair that slammed against the fence.

I began to piece together the situation. Matt was confronting her. And he wasn't holding anything back. I tried to focus on what was happening.

Alana - Awakening

I was too tired too open my eyes. My limbs heavy with sleep, I lay

still and listened to my soft breathing. Exhaustion weighed me down.

I didn't bother to think of anything in that moment. I was trapped in a

limbo between sleeping and waking.

Opening my eyes, I stared at the blackness that swam in

front of me. My legs ached like I hadn't slept. The more I forced

myself awake, the more a heavy dizziness set in. I was drinking, so it

was expected of course, considering the large amount of alcohol I

had likely consumed throughout the previous night. Looking around

the darkness that my eyes had yet to adjust to, I concluded that it was

likely the middle of the night or early morning. The only feeling I

could muster at that point was the immediate, quickening pace of my

heart.

I felt a dull pain behind my eyes that radiated through my

skull. It was a good indication that I was experiencing a hangover. It

was also the sign of a good night, a regrettable night, but good one

nonetheless. I tried to recall a

memory of the night before but my mind blurred. I was unable to process anything.

My eyes still hadn't adjusted to the thick darkness that surrounded the room. In that moment, I figured it was because I was in someone's room. Maybe Matt's; hopefully Matt's. Sighing, I tried to push away the anxious feeling that was growing in my chest. I wriggled my feet and pins and needles shot up my feet towards my legs.

Breathing heavily, I wriggled my hands that were at my sides by my hips. My hands were numb. Alarmed, I strained to move them. Painful pins and needles shot through my hands and up my arms. I realized why the circulation was cut off to my hands - I was tied up.

Lightheaded, and forcing myself to continue breathing, I tried to keep my wits about me. I writhed my wrists back and fourth against the rope. Panic shot through my chest. Being restrained was one of my worst fears.

My heart beat quickened, just as my breathing did. Like clockwork, adrenalin set in and rang like alarms all over my body. My instincts told me to *get up.* But the circumstances I was in worked against it. The feeling made me sick with dread.

The realization that something wasn't right hit me so fast; I had no time to think, no time to plan. My only thought was that somebody had taken me here to kill me, rape me or both. At that moment, all I wanted to do was run, to see some sort of sunlight at the very least, just to know I was still alive. I was starting to get dizzy and delusional.

Gulping on thick, humid air, I strained to move my hands. They wriggled just like they normally would, but when I tried to lift my arms up they wouldn't budge more than a millimeter. The ropes were tighter than I could get out of.

Logic was slipping away. With the realization that something wasn't right here, my brain was turning to mush. Although I racked my brain for ideas to get out of this, I couldn't seem to think.

A sickening feeling rolled through my stomach, making my heart jump into my throat. I ached with panic, the type of panic I had never felt before, the type of panic that was impossible to subside.

"Oh my god," I whispered, breathing hard. Throwing myself forward in unnerved motion, I noticed how thin the rope was, it gave me a sense of hope because my initial thought was I could tear through them, but that was unrealistic and my train of thought was exploding with impractical possibilities.

My blood pulsed evenly throughout my body making my fingers hot. My chest began to ache. The impact of throwing myself forward in the ropes did nothing, except make me acutely aware of the thin ropes slashing into my wrists.

Cursing, I tried to sit up in a calm manner while wincing at the rope rubbing against my fresh wounds. It was hard not to panic. I knew panicking would get me nowhere, but it was human instinct. I had two options, one of which to scream until I couldn't anymore and the other to try to slip out of the restraints without making a noise and find an escape without having the possibility of the person who tied me up returning for me. Option number two seemed more appealing, however, it felt as if I couldn't calm myself down enough to try.

My mind tried to calm down my body, but my heart was beating too fast, my throat aching too much, my body shaking in tremors.

The fact that it was so dark worried me. I couldn't see what was around me or where I was or how to get out. The darkness always did calm me, but this time the circumstances were different. Nothing seemed to calm me down. I knew that something wasn't right. Maybe it was intuition or maybe my mind had blocked what had happened to me, but here I was, trying to understand just what was going on.

I wanted to rub my eyes in frustration in attempt to see anything. Maybe the person who tied me up in here was still in the room.

Another tremor of fright rolled up my spine. Frustrated, I shook my head. There was no point in getting worked up over something that wasn't happening. *Keep calm,* I reminded myself. Swallowing a scream, I tried my best to keep quiet. Screaming would only make things worse, and I wasn't mentally prepared for anything worse than what I was already dealing with.

I didn't remember much from before I was caught. All I seemed to be able to remember is useless information like the taste of vodka, Matt's anger, Tanya's jealousy, and the party spiraling out of control. My mind wasn't cooperating but I was desperate for answers. Tears of frustration sprung to my eyes. I couldn't understand why all I was thinking of was how I had gotten here and not how to get out.

I have to get out of here, I realized, trembling. Whoever had attacked me might be back soon. Soon could mean anything, it could mean one minute or a day. Panicked, I started to writhe my wrists, the rope biting into the tender flesh on my wrists.

The ropes held tight, but my frustration was getting worse, and the pain in my chest ached with dread.

Stressing the rope, I pulled, and pulled, the backs of my hands raw with rope burn. I couldn't wait. I wouldn't wait. I needed to get out *now*. I started to slam forward in the ropes, panic hitting me harder than before. A scream of shock escaped my throat. Warm blood started to trickle down my arms towards my up-turned palms.

It wasn't supposed to happen like this. I had so much life left to live.

What about my family? The question rang through my head in panic. I twisted my arms toward my torso at the thought. The rope burned my arms every millimeter I moved. The only thought fuelling me was I had to get out of there. The blood that had trickled all over my hands were sticky when I balled my fists.

Angry, I threw myself forward in the chair, the ropes slicing into my wounded wrists. I screamed in agony, and then fell back, feeling helpless. Maybe I was going to die after all. Maybe there was no way I could get out. Panic rose in my chest. Throwing myself forward, I tried to wriggle the ropes off my wrists. Finally freeing my hand, I scraped at the other to get it loose.

My paranoia wasn't going to go away until I was out of the shed and free. Lightheaded, I stumbled toward the door and fell into it. I was so close. Slowly, I crept down. I spotted a knife that was on the floor of the shed. It was old that's for sure, it was discolored with a silver handle. Examining the tip, I lifted it to my hand. It would be useful in case someone came back for me. Squeezing the handle into my palm, I waited.

I opened the door and surveyed the area outside of the shed. It was the woods Ivy and I used to play in as kids and it was right by our house. It was a creepy place to wake up in but I didn't have time to ask questions. I had to get out.

I stumbled out and fell onto the ground in shock. Although my mind was pushing me to move forward, my body wasn't willing to cooperate. I took the time to try to catch my breath and think about what had just happened.

The sun was still hiding behind the horizon, lighting the forest in a cool, early morning blue. Gasping for breath, my lungs ached in shock at the cold air.

My eyes caught sight of the rubble behind me. The shed was gone. In its place was a pile of ash and metal objects. What wasn't logically possible was sitting right in front of my eyes. "What the fuck," I muttered, drinking in the sight in front of me. Stumbling on my feet, I walked over to the black shards that inhabited the place where the old shed was. None of this was making sense. I had just stumbled out of a shed that was there literally five seconds ago. And now it was gone.

Maybe I am dead. That thought flashed through my mind but I tried to push it aside without any luck. Maybe I was reliving the old memories I had before I had died and that's why everything was collaborating together like this. That was my only "logical" thought and even that didn't make much sense.

Trying hard to dig up memories, I ran my fingers through my tangled hair. All I could think of was the useless information of the party like the cool taste of my drink against my lips. Why was that all I could remember? I remembered Tanya being a bitch, which was normal behavior for her. I didn't see much of my best friend Angela, she was too busy drinking up the single life and flirting with the guys at the party. Why did I remember all of these things but not the important questions like what the fuck was I doing here in the middle of nowhere, and why the hell was that shed that I just stumbled out of now burnt the ground?

Noticing the ground was coated in frost, I lifted my left stiletto up in shock. Painfully aware of my shoes, I peeled them off and unveiled my bare feet. Cringing, I lifted my foot up; it was covered in the melting frost and dirt, which created a muddy, grimy feeling on my soles.

It was time to go home. It was all too much for me to take in. I maneuvered my way through the woods back to Gran and grandpa's house, stepping on my tippy toes and hoping to god not to step in dog shit. This awakening was already too rough for me.

I slipped in through the side-door. It was early morning so I hoped not to wake anyone. Noticing the vacant bathroom, I let out a sigh of relief and took a run for it.

The hot water scalded my fresh wounds. As I tried not to cringe, I worked at the blood on my arms that ran from my wrists to my elbows. No matter how hard I scrubbed the dried blood wouldn't come off of my skin. I scratched at it a bit more before giving up. The amount of blood at the bottom of the half-clogged shower drain was almost nauseating. I couldn't believe that a few rope-burns on the wrists would cause that much blood, but there it was, swirling toward the drain, crimson in color. Confused, I examined my cuts closer. They weren't coming clean. They must have already clotted.

When I stepped out of the shower, and dressed, I examined my wrists closer. The burns looked more like slashes but I guess that was expected.

I turned to look in the full-length mirror. I was wearing the same outfit I was wearing when I woke up the first time. Why the hell would I put my dirty clothes with blood all over them back on? That wouldn't make sense, even if I was hung over.

Squinting at myself in the mirror, I began to shiver. Red blood spurted from the blue fabric over my abdomen, it leaked onto the floor, dripping over my bare feet and spreading over the linoleum floor. Gasping, I jumped back.

Looking back to the mirror, I stared into my horrified expression, then back at the floor. It was clean. My feet were clean. I looked up at my stomach. Grasped it. All I felt was the fabric under my fingers. There was no red, no blood.

What the hell was wrong with me?

Confused, I stumbled out of the washroom into my room and started digging through my drawers. I looked up into the mirror, surveying my face as I continued to shake in tremors.

Suddenly a scream shattered the stillness of my room and I leaped high into the air with shock. I looked behind me, half in anger half in surprise. "Jesus, was that necessary?" I snapped at Ivy in the mirror. "You scared the hell out of me. I know my clothes are dirty and I need to change but what an overreaction," I growled, turning back around to tend to my outfit. Something different about her caught my eye in the mirror. Slowly, I turned around and faced my sister.

It was definitely her despite the fact that she looked completely different. Her mousy hair was tamed and a lot longer than she liked to keep it. She seemed different then when I last saw her... but that didn't make any sense. She wouldn't have changed overnight. Even if I had been gone a couple of days, even a week, she wouldn't have changed this much. She looked strikingly...like me. I had never seen the resemblance until now.

"Are you wearing makeup?" I scoffed, peering at her with squinted eyes.

Ivy seemed to have stopped breathing. She fell back into the hallway, her back pressed against the wall. "No, no, no," she whispered to herself, as if the repetition soothed her.

"Chill, everyone wears makeup," I laughed.

When she didn't respond, I peaked out of the doorway. "Okay, should I be worried? Did you overdose on cocaine or something?" Normally I would have laughed at that but couldn't find it in me.

Ivy's eyes widened at the sight of me again. She slid down the wall, dramatizing her reaction.

"I'll take that as a no?" Silence. Rolling my eyes up at the ceiling, I waited for a second longer but still she refused to speak.

Ivy glanced up at me through her splayed fingers across her eyes. She looked like a frightened child, her eyes widening with every passing second. Tears glinted in her dark eyes.

"Ivy," I reached for her face but coughed out a laugh instead, "you look like you shit your pants!" I couldn't help it; her face was priceless. It was probably insensitive for me to make a joke when my sister was in emotional turmoil over the sight of me. Usually, I was the one in emotional turmoil over the sight of *her*.

"Wow, it's really you," Ivy gasped through tears.

Kinking my eyebrows, I stared at her in amusement, trying to come up with a sarcastic comment but my eyes fell upon my wrists and I lost my train of thought. "Okay, this is a little ridiculous, maybe I look bad but I'm alive, and the way you're acting is… beginning to scare me."

"It's not that," Ivy said, her eyes burning into mine. She then looked down into her lap, "you've been missing for months."

"What are you talking about?" I snapped, "I'm here, aren't I?"

She didn't respond.

My stomach shifted. I had a bad feeling about this. I had no idea what my sister was talking about... It was the type of circumstance that caused shivers to roll down my spine. She had to be confused. There was no other logical explanation. That, or she is dealing with a mental illness. Either way, I felt inclined to look after her. She was my sister, and despite how much I really hated her at times, I owed her that.

Frowning, I leaned forward trying to grasp Ivy's shoulders' in attempt to make eye contact, but she refused to look at me, her dark eyes darting everywhere around the room but at me. I wanted to reassure her, like I failed to do when we were younger. She just always seemed like she was fine and she never needed anything. Something about her had changed, something I couldn't quite see. I didn't know how to help her.

Circumstances were different and it was more like I had to reassure her it was okay to be crazy and there are treatments out there to make it seem like she hadn't completely lost it.

"I'm here, I'm alive," I said. "What exactly is wrong with you?"

She fixed her gaze upon me, "I'm not crazy," she said, gridding her teeth in anger.

"Of course not," I said, "But I mean, really," I shrugged, "I'm here." Everything looked real. Everything seemed real… so everything had to be real. That or I was in a dream that I would wake up from soon. It would make more sense if it were a dream.

Ivy stared at me a second longer before breaking into heavy tears, messy tears.

"I was only gone a day or two," I murmured, making deliberate eye contact with my sister, hoping to find answers in her eyes.

Ivy shook her head, the look on her face telling me I was far-off. "Alana, it's been three months."

Shaking my head, I peered into her eyes looking for evidence that she was lying. This was ridiculous; there was no way I was gone for three months; maybe three days, but not three months.

"Okay now you're beginning to freak me out." Gasping for air, I looked around my room, thinking of the very possibility of my sister being right. She seemed to know more than I did. My eyes darted around my room, looking for something to match Ivy's explanation.

Everything looked the exact way I had left it the night before the party. My straightener was sitting on the wooden dresser, the hairspray knocked over, just the way I left it; in a hurry for the party. Clothes scattered around the clothes hamper the way I always left it. "If I'm really dead why is my room the way I left it?" I asked.

Ivy looked down in silence, her eyes darting back and forth, as if she was in a weird trance. She murmured to herself softly, her eyes flickering from left to right.

Scowling, I spun around and started for the door. "This is freaking me out, I'm going to go talk to Gran," I claimed, without bothering to look back at the blank look on Ivy's face. I stomped out of the room leaving Ivy to her own messed up confusion.

I hadn't seen Ivy react that way since I was ten, when our parents had died. Ever since then, Ivy was a nervous pushover; she had little to no people skills and was always the shy, sweet one. It was annoying to be the one expected to take charge. I liked being in control but I didn't want to deal with my sisters' mental breakdown over nothing. Running down the stairs, I spotted Gran standing outside the side door, a cup of tea in her hands.

Bursting through the door, I stood right in front of her.

"Gran," I snapped breathless, "Ivy told me I went missing but it's fine, I'm here. But when Ivy saw me she started acting really weird, like I don't think she even knows what is going on and it's freaking me out. I think we should take her to the hospital."

Gran continued to stare off into the woods, a far-off look in her eyes, as if she were searching for something... Maybe me. That thought sent shivers spiraling up my spine. Ignoring the thought, I continued my explanation.

"She either overdosed on drugs, which is ridiculous because it seems really out of character for her. I don't know but she has it in her mind that I'm dead and honestly, I can't deal with it."

Gran sipped from her light blue cup gingerly, her eyes still vacant as if I hadn't said anything at all. My voice didn't shock her, and my stern tone did nothing. She didn't even look at me.

"Seriously?" I asked, taken aback. "You're going to ignore me?" I laughed a tense laugh and then stepped back. "Why are you ignoring me? Is this your idea of punishment or something? I was at a party and I don't know how I was gone so long, I really don't." I didn't want to accept the fact that Gran hadn't even realized my presence.

Gran pressed her hand on her lower back, wincing at the pain. Gaining her posture, she turned around and walked toward me. And then through me. Gasping is shock, I lurched back against the door. Gran threw the screen door open and walked through me again just a moment after.

Breathing heavy in shock, I stayed pushed up against the door in horror. There was no way to explain what had just happened. Despite the fact it did happen, I chose not to think about it and followed Gran through the door.

The sharp sound of the phone rang hollow through my racing thoughts.

Gran answered the phone. "Hello?" She asked her voice rising with hope. She stood in the middle of the kitchen, her eyes seemed to light up with hope. Then her expression fell. "I won't give up. I expect the same from this organization," she looked around the room, her expression seeming to fall more. "I realize that, but it's been 94 days and there's still a chance. I think we should be actively looking for her... Yes I know it's been three months but... Maybe we could do another search party..."

I figured they were talking about me, whoever she was talking to.

"Yes, I'm aware of that but why would you or anyone else give up on a child? Whether or not you are willing to help, we will find her... or at least her body for god sakes, this has torn my family apart and I will not give up. She needs to come home where she belongs. We can't set up a funeral without a body, she would think we're giving up on her and we won't do that. Please give us a little more time!"

My breath caught in my throat. *A body*. I was aware this wasn't a joke now. This was too far and too much to take in. Choking on my breath, I fell against the wall and stood there, trying to keep my body from shaking.

"Well some organization you are," Gran scoffed, red creeping from her neck to her face. It was one way you could tell Gran was really angry. I had caused her to look at me like that when I snuck in and she was up, but it was different hearing about the news of my death and how that angered her.

Gran huffed into the phone as if trying to control her frustration. "If you're not making a profit off of the story you are no longer interested. You know, I have already lost my daughter and my son-in-law, I really don't need to lose my granddaughter too," she cried, tears glistening in her eyes.

Slamming down the phone, Gran stared at it for a second before breaking into soft sobs that started off with tears bursting from her eyes. She fell forward, her face in her hands. Out of a burst of anger, Gran pushed the phone off of the counter where it was sitting. The batteries fell out and rolled on the floor, one rolled toward me. Staring at it in omniscient silence I read the battery name over and over. *Duracell Duracell Duracell.* It was the only thing that would keep me from crying at the sight of my grandmother withering toward the floor in tears.

Grandpa walked through the door at that second, the screen door snapping against the doorframe. He walked into the kitchen, and at the sight of Gran, dropped two paper bags of groceries on the counter and rushed to her side. I caught Ivy's eyes from down the hall, staring in shock at Gran. Grandpa knelt down and rested his hand on Gran's upper back. He didn't have to say anything. Gran turned and buried her face into his neck, heaving and sobbing.

I couldn't help but notice the connection and love between my grandparents, the type of thing I would never take notice of when I was alive. They didn't even have to speak, they knew each other so completely. It was something I hadn't picked up on. And the sad part about that is, when I was alive, I didn't even notice it, because I expected to live. I expected to see the day where I too would feel that connection with someone, to grow old with someone. Expectations have a way of letting you down.

Robeline – Chasing ghosts

Silence swallowed the room. My words were sinking into Robeline's brain and she didn't seem to register them. I blinked at her expectantly, waiting for a response, for anything. I could almost see the gears turning in her head, processing what I had just poured out to her.

"Alana showed up three months after she went missing," Robeline stated, her tone flat. She averted her eyes from me, and scribbled what I had said down on her notepad. She looked up with me, "Nobody else could see her because she was... a ghost." She struggled with the word, pausing expectantly. She thought I was crazy. This reaction was expected and although I knew that it angered me to see her act so unprofessional about it.

"This is why I don't tell people this," I snapped, "Because people automatically think I'm crazy," I waved my hands in the air as an exaggeration. It was precisely what I wanted to avoid telling Robeline specifically because I expected that exact response. But my story didn't fit without it.

Frustrated, I started to snap the sole on my shoe again, it echoed through the room. It was becoming a habit because I was trapped in this tomb and forced to talk about feelings.

"I'm just trying to piece together what happened here, I'm sorry if it looks like I'm having a hard time grasping this, I'm just trying to gather information the exact way you're telling it to me and you do have to admit that seeing a ghost is a little… strange," Robeline reasoned. "And could you please stop doing that?" She asked, referring to the sole of my shoe slapping against the linoleum.

Forcing a deep breath, I stopped and glared at Robeline. Sitting in overwhelming silence, I became acutely aware of all of the sounds that the office-like cubicle made. The buzzing of the florescent light above me hit my brain like a sledgehammer. It was hard to think with a noise like that bouncing off the walls in the tiny room. The longer the droning continued, the more it angered me.

"Did you follow Alana a lot?" Robeline asked, tapping her pen on the notebook. She looked me over but the look on her face told me she already knew the answer. Not that it mattered; the question was irrelevant except for the fact that it made me look weird.

"What does that matter?" I muttered, scowling. "I mean

95

really, even if I did, how does that have anything to do with what I'm going through?"

Robeline glared at me, hard. It was clear she was getting frustrated with my response, however, I had said enough for her to start writing on her notepad.

"What is your relationship with alcohol?" Robeline asked, her eyes averted from mine.

"My relationship?" I scoffed. She didn't respond. "Does it really ask that?"

Robeline looked up at me through her glasses, her expression showing blatant irritation.

"That was my first party," I said.

"Right, I got that," Robeline said. "What I meant was 'do you have a substance abuse problem?'"

"No," I said, falling back into my chair and crossing my arms.

Robeline glared at me. "I will need you to answer these questions honestly."

"When I drink, I go hard," I said, "Then I started to rely on it, I guess you can say. I wouldn't say it's much of a problem. I just didn't know how else to deal with my sister. It was an automatic release for me."

"Do you still drink?" Robeline asked.

"No."

"Do you struggle with depression?"

"What?" I demanded, shifting in my seat.

"Sometimes people turn to alcohol because of depression or loneliness. Although, depression can also be a result of feeling alone with your thoughts and ideas. Do you feel alone a lot of the time?"

Scowling, I made deliberate eye contact with Robeline. I hated the way she spoke to me like a child. "I don't feel comfortable answering that."

Robeline nodded and checked a box on her spreadsheet.

"What did you write down about me?" I demanded, leaning forward in an attempt to make out the small letters. "That I'm delusional?"

Robeline ignored me, but made it obvious that she was uncomfortable with the question as her hand clamped her pen.

"Relax, I'm not going to fight you for it," I offered, leaning forward, "I'm just curious as to what you're writing down. Because I can assure you that she was there. And maybe you don't believe in spirits and how they can communicate with you but I know I'm not crazy. This happened. Believe me, I was just as shocked as you are right now hearing this." Of course my reasoning sounded stupid. Cringing, I stretched and turned my attention to the window.

"I'm just writing down what you are telling me," Robeline stated.

Ivy – Sleepless nights

I saw Alana. It was her, exactly how I had remembered her. Nothing had changed. Nothing apart from her memory. She had no recollection of what had happened to her. I wondered if she would ever remember.

My eyes were shut but my thoughts were racing, a sure sign that sleeping would be impossible.

Opening my eyes, I stared at the grooves in the ceiling above my bed. There was no way I would fall asleep, even if I were able to calm my mind. I kept drifting back to the night Alana went missing and the last time I saw her. Alana was right. I shouldn't have gotten involved. I should have stayed home that night.

My mind racing with thoughts, I reached for the melatonin I kept at my bedside; the only way I would ever make it through the night.

I couldn't help but struggle with the idea of telling someone about Alana returning, not even knowing she had passed on. It was weighing on me, but telling someone wasn't an option. It would make me sound crazy and I really couldn't blame anyone for thinking that I was. That, and it would upset Gran who had been through too much already. She had aged more in these past few months than she had since my mother died. Her life was falling apart around her, and she wasn't the only one. I knew that I was going to struggle with the beginning of another insomnia battle.

My anxiety began to rise again, causing my heart to race and my breathing to become irregular. The all-to-familiar panic rose inside me. Heart palpitations. All I could hear was my heartbeat in my ears. The second I recognized my heart racing, I began to panic about panicking. Sitting up in bed, I forced a deep, shaky breath in an attempt to subside the feeling.

My thoughts raced. Memories. God, so many memories that seemed to flash back into my mind the second I saw Alana again. They were more like dreams. Like she wasn't ever really here. She had so many dreams and aspirations; it was something I admired of her. Even though I never really questioned her dreams I remember asking her why she would ever want to deal with blood and surgeries, and all I could remember was her grinning at me, and saying "I want to help people, silly. Obviously, I don't want to see blood and guts, but can you imagine saving someone's life? It would make me feel like I was making a difference in the world."

I can still remember Alana watching surgeries on TV, sipping strong coffee from her Lake Louise mug. She cherished that thing but would never admit it. Her eyes were fixed to the television set, almost as if she was worried she might miss something important, that puzzle piece that fixed the entire picture in place. Then she would turn to me and smile, her hair up in a messy morning bun, her blond hair glistening in the sun that was pouring in through the window. That was one of the rare times she treated me with kindness but I held on to that memory more than I like to admit. It illuminated the good side of her. Too bad she wasn't like that all the time.

Alana's bad side out weighed her good. Deep down there was something more to her that not a lot of people saw, or put the effort in to see. I knew more about Alana than anyone. I saw a lot of her change when our parents died. I couldn't quite tell if that triggered the change or if it was something else, but all of the sudden she didn't want anything to do with me.

She just changed, but there was that little part of her that I wished would come back. But that's the thing, there was no way for me to know if she had changed for good. That the old her was dead, or, maybe, if I was patient, she would come back. There was also the idea that I was naive and stupid for thinking that. That once a person changes, they're different and there's no sense in praying for them to come back.

I fell back into the bed, and rolled over to glance at the alarm clock - 2:20AM. It blinked at me, a reminder that I had yet to fix it the last time the power went out. I was out of sorts. Clicking on the screen of my phone, I saw the actual time, 1:44AM.

I was wired and the more I tossed and turned, the more it finalized my fate for the night. I sat up in bed. It was apparent to me that sleep was a battle that I just wouldn't win. My mind was racing too much and there was no point in getting frustrated over not sleeping. I swung my legs out of bed and started for the kitchen.

The silence of the house was overwhelming. My footsteps seemed to pad loudly through the house and the last thing I wanted was attention right now. I didn't need to be questioned on why I wasn't sleeping.

Clicking the kettle on, I took out a mug without looking. When my eyes fell on it I realized it was Alana's favorite mug. Studying it, I recalled the memory I had earlier. My hand hovering over the mug, I struggled with internal conflict.

It wasn't like anyone would see anyway. I reached for a bag of chamomile tea and closed the cupboard quietly, hoping not to wake anyone because the house was dead silent.

Chamomile was the best tea for relaxation, Gran swore on it. Even if I weren't going to get rest I did have to try to relax my mind and body so I would feel a little better by morning.

Gran stumbled into the kitchen. It was obvious she had given up on sleep as well. She was wearing her blue pajama set, the white sleeves wrinkled by what I thought was tears. "Can't sleep?" she asked, pulling out a mug and placing it on the counter.

Shaking my head, I sat down at the kitchen table.

Gran glanced at my mug. "It feels like she's everywhere," she murmured.

I questioned whether I should tell gran what I had seen. I questioned it even though I knew it was the stupidest thing to question and I'd already thought about it over and over. I mulled over the issue because the more I didn't say anything, the more it weighed on me, suffocated me. I didn't want to make her more emotional. Or worse yet, have her think I was making something up or that there was something wrong with me. The mention of Alana's name would make me sick to my stomach anyway.

"You look pale," Gran observed, peering at me through red-rimmed eyes.

"I'm fine," I said, shaking my head, "but you don't look so good."

Gran sighed, her breath rattling through her lungs. "They've given up looking for Alana," her voice cracked at her name, and I looked down automatically, as if I hadn't already known that.

The kettle started to whistle from the corner, subtle at first and then loud. Instantly, I stood up to retrieve it, anything to get away from the conversation we were having. Pouring the hot liquid into both of our cups, I watched as the tea bags bounced back and fourth.

I wondered if we would ever move past this or if Alana's absence would haunt us forever. At that moment, it felt like there was no moving on. I was trying to turn the page but everyone else was still stuck on the last chapter. There was nothing more frustrating than that.

Alana - Crushed

"You've gotta be fucking kidding me," I muttered to myself.

Angela was in Matt's apartment? Alone? I was pressed up against the window to Matt's apartment. He lived on the bottom floor of an apartment complex, and it made for a decent view of all of the cars driving by. It was shitty, but cheap.

Angela was sitting on the couch, a beer in her pale hand. Since when did Angela drink beer? Scowling, I squinted my eyes, desperate to find someone else in the apartment. Matt sauntered out of the washroom and collapsed on the couch beside Angela. He leaned forward and touched her face.

My heart stopped as he leaned further and kissed her. His eyes drifted to the window.

Gasping, I spun around out of sight, my back against the cement wall. I struggled to catch my breath. My boyfriend and my best friend were... *dating*? They even looked *happy,* as stupid as that was.

He should have been

mourning. Did I mean nothing to him? It felt as if someone was clenching my heart in their hand, squeezing so hard every beat of my heart ached and rattled against my chest. Every breath hurt. My heart ached.

Not that I even had a heart anymore considering I was dead or in purgatory or whatever this prison was. Curious, I peaked through the window again. Matt was taking off Angela's sweater. They were fully making out now. It was so painful, I wanted nothing more than to look away, yet I was so transfixed I couldn't bring myself to move.

If I had a stomach, I may have puked.

My throat clenched as I continued to stare. I felt pathetic. I was getting tired of having emotions. So that was what it felt like to be heartbroken. Hot tears sprang to my eyes and I didn't even bother to wipe them away because it would take too much effort. It was like I was giving into my weakness, not caring if I felt stupid.

I stared into the darkening sky as I slid down the wall, crumpling to the ground in exaggerated exhaustion from the scene inside. It felt like every muscle in my body had given up and turned to mush.

Looking down at my feet, I noticed frost had already begun

to build up on the surface of the thin blades of grass. It was fucking cold outside. Why in the hell was I still able to feel pain and irritation if I was dead? Wasn't I supposed to feel nothing? It would be so easy to feel nothing.

In that moment, I wished Matt could feel the agony that I felt, as selfish as that was to think. All that we were was gone in three months. How was that even possible? I think the worst part of all of this was that the people I trusted and held dearest to me had all moved on and I was stuck. I had lost everything that had ever meant anything to me. What was I left with? Not even my life. More tears gushed to my eyes and I didn't care to wipe them away.

Naturally, I tried to think of anything good in this situation. But there was nothing. There was maybe the slim chance I wasn't dead and maybe this was all just a fucking nightmare. The pain that I felt was too real for that thought to even be a question.

All of the people I loved and cared about had forgotten about me or moved on. As if I were nothing to them. At one time I used to believe *I* was so *important*.

I didn't really know what I expected to happen in the span of three months. I guess I just had this picture in my mind that people would still be broken over me and that maybe they would still be looking for me and that maybe I would cross their minds every now and again, and maybe I was feeling this way because I would do that for them. I would do all of that for them and they didn't do any of that for me.

I started to think about how I treated people when I was here. Maybe that's why they didn't miss me. But it's not like I can take back how I acted and it's not like I could change what was different now. I would forever be living in regret because nothing was how I thought it would be. And finally my actions had caught up with me.

Some lesson that was, I thought as I turned back to the window, my heart dropping again. I felt empty. I had lost everything that I ever was. I was blank.

Ivy – It's not right

Taking in my appearance, I stood back from the mirror.

The wings of my eyeliner finally looked even - I had mastered the shake in my hand. My eye shadow looked decent as well, even though I didn't blend it properly. There were no longer dark circles under my eyes despite my lack of sleep.Finally, I was able to contour my face the way Alana had been able to when she was around. It was weird to think I was using her makeup while she was gone… I had never really felt the need to use it before but I couldn't understand why. Makeup seemed to empower me.

It was strange how, at one time, I was scared of it. Just a few months ago, I walked around with invisible eyelashes and dark circles under my eyes. No wonder no one could see the resemblance between Alana and I. Even though we shared a washroom for our whole lives, I almost felt ashamed to follow in her footsteps. Yet we shared a house at one time. That was it. Until now, of course.

My eyes wandered into the shower and I noticed that I was getting low on shampoo. I made a mental note to pick some up next time I was to go to the drug store. Maybe this time I would pick a scent that wasn't so nauseating.

Turning back to the mirror, I stared into my dark eyes, and tilted my head. Why couldn't I just have a lighter eye color? All I wanted was blue eyes. They were just so beautiful. Instead I was stuck with brown. Everything was brown. I was stuck with my father's features.

Sighing, I lifted the hot iron to the top of my head. My hair straightened with ease, leaving it longer and smoother. Almost perfect.

I walked to my dresser and pulled open the second drawer. My clothes were beginning to become a letdown. It felt like I had nothing to wear. Nonetheless, I had to put something on and I picked a white button up shirt. Carefully, I pressed the buttons through the holes, not breaking eye contact with my dark eyes in the mirror above my dresser.

Studying myself, insults popped into my mind. It was like Alana was taunting me. I still wasn't good enough. In fact, I looked like I was ready to go to work and I didn't even have a job. Why did I even wear button up shirts? I remembered buying it. It was on sale. Everything I bought was on sale. The more aware of this fact I became, the more I began to realize that there was usually a reason why they were on sale. Take for example my white button down shirt. It was made of cotton and sat awkwardly against my chest, spewing out near my stomach area, making me look bigger than I really was. It was a bad fit.

Digging through my drawers, I pulled out shirt after shirt. The blue tank top I pulled out had loose strings hanging from the seam; that was on sale. The over-sized T-shirt with a lion in it was enormous and made me look bigger. Sighing in frustration, I looked at my reflection again. Maybe it was time to change my style. Or lack there of, considering the fact I had absolutely no sense of style. Where would I even begin? Would it be wrong if I borrowed something from Alana's closet? Would that be weird? It's not like she could wear her clothes anymore and she did have excellent taste.

After debating with myself for what felt like forever, I started to unbutton the white shirt.

I tiptoed toward Alana's room down the hall. The door was closed as I expected. The pain was too much for Gran and grandpa. In a sudden hurry, I ran up the hall and peaked into the living room. I couldn't hear or see anyone. I stood silent for another moment. There still wasn't any shuffling or talking. Not even the drone of the TV.

They had gone out. I was safe.

Walking back to Alana's room, I cracked the door open.

It was exactly how Alana had left it, clothes were scattered everywhere. A spray can of hairspray was left knocked over on her dresser. I picked it up and pushed it to the back of the dresser. Examining my face in the mirror, I cringed at my clothes again. I needed Alana's help, I was sure she would understand. I would even make a point to explain it to her the next time I saw her. It wasn't like she could tell me no anyway.

I started to dig through her drawers one by one, grabbing anything that looked visually appealing. Then I noticed her perfume on the dresser. I spritzed myself, inhaling the sweet hibiscus floral scent and then continued digging through her drawers.

~

Laying on the couch, I focused on the steady clicking of the large clock on the wall. I didn't notice the sound until then. I didn't even know it made a sound. The repetition was soothing and predictable. I couldn't decide if I hated it or found it comforting.

My eyelids were heavy, and my mind began to drift. It was a wonder how I was still unable to sleep.

Someone knocked on the door. It was quiet, barely audible.

Sitting up, I knotted my fingers together and looked toward the door. I could see Angela behind the door, her angelic face peeking through the glass. *Why do people do that? It is the creepiest thing.* Sighing, I started toward the door.

Opening the door, I revealed Angela's timid face.

"Hi Angela," I said, forcing a smile. "How are you?" I didn't care.

"Hey Ivy," Angela smiled and then looked down at the ground. "I wanted to talk to you about the other night, if that's alright?"

"Of course," I said. Realizing it was probably more appropriate to invite her in, I moved to the side, and welcomed her in. She walked in and slid off her turquoise flats. She tugged at her purse, and then decided to leave it on.

"Been awhile since I've been here," Angela laughed and toyed with her short hair. She wound it around her finger over and over. I knew I wouldn't like whatever she had to say.

I didn't respect what she had to say. It wasn't like she came around after Alana had gone missing either. I guess nobody did.

It had been awhile but in a way it felt like just yesterday she was over here with my sister, fighting over the mirror in my sisters room.

"Well, come in," I said, motioning to the living room. It was an awkward place to talk but where else would I talk with my dead sisters best friend? I didn't particularly want her in my house to begin with, yet there she was. All because I was too nice to just have ignored her knock.

I took a seat on the couch and watched as Angela surveyed the place, her face emotionless. It was weird to see her so tense and nervous when for years, Alana and her would lounge around on the couches and watch movies. Maybe my presence was too much. After Alana had gone missing, I didn't see Angela anymore. But then again, what did I expect after her best friend had died. It's not like she would have stopped in to see me.

Angela looked down the hallway and then back the other way, catching a glimpse of herself in the mirror. "Wow, I didn't realize there were so many mirrors in this place."

Barking a laugh, I looked around, "Well considering Alana lived here, are you really shocked?"

Angela gave me a half smile, and walked up to the couch across from me before taking a seat on the edge of the couch. It looked more like she was squatting. "Looks like you guys remodeled a little," she commented, her eyes darted around the unfamiliar space.

"Yeah a little," I said, praying she would stop talking about the house. "We had to change it around because everything kept reminding us of…" I paused, trying to think of the proper word for what had happened to Alana.

Angela nodded knowingly, "So I think you know why I'm here," she said, looking down.

"No, not really," I lied, tilting my head to the side. My opinion was already out there, there was no need for me to talk about it more. There was really no need for her to be at my house. "Was there something you wanted to talk about?" I asked, enjoying the confusion that crossed Angela's eyes.

"It's just, you really seemed upset by the news of," she took a deep breath, "Matt and I. It bothered me because I want you to know that it is nothing serious, he was there to help me cope in a time when I really needed somebody and vice versa," she rambled, splaying her hands open on her lap, "And I guess we kind of just developed a relationship, but I really don't want something like that to bother you. Like I said, it's really nothing serious." She looked up at me, waiting for a response.

"Then why are you dating?" I asked, squinted my eyes at her. I wanted nothing more than to trip her up on her obviously rehearsed speech. I began to pick apart her appearance as my hatred multiplied.

She took a deep breath as if caught in a lie and continued. "It's just... He really helped me through a lot and we really leaned on each other through this whole process."

"Shouldn't you have been mourning my sister instead of growing 'feelings' for each other?" I asked dumbly, enjoying the way she stumbled over what she was saying.

"I just came over here to say that if it really bothers you so much Ivy, we won't date," She cringed as if hoping to god I would allow it. "I mean, you are right. It is kind of disrespectful. Alana has only been missing for a few months and it is a little soon I guess."

Nodding, I bit my lower lip and turned toward the noisy clock. Watching the hands of the clock away, I tried to come up with what to say next. But I didn't know what to say. I wanted to say, yeah it's completely disrespectful and you two shouldn't be thinking of dating right now but at the same time it really wasn't my place to say anything. I was only the sister of the girl involved in this tragedy.

"You know, it's not really my place," I said, averting my

gaze from the clock. "I just don't get it. I don't get how you grow feelings for each other out of mourning his dead girlfriend and your dead best friend." My words stung Angela, which was the exact reaction I was looking for.

"We don't know she's dead yet," Angela claimed, hope and just a hint of dread hanging in her blue eyes. She seemed to ignore what I had said otherwise as if I had embarrassed her by revealing what she was actually doing.

"If she weren't, she'd be pissed," I said, hanging her feeling of dread out in plain view. "So I guess you better hope she is." Too far. Shit.

"Are you serious?" Angela asked, narrowing her eyes at me.

"I'm just saying," I claimed, trying to reason with my outburst, "By the way, it's a little weird. If you'd ask me, it's extremely suspicious."

"What, you think I have something to do with Alana's disappearance?" Angela asked, her eyes narrowing.

"Well I don't know," I shrugged, leaning forward. "My sister goes missing mysteriously and then all of the sudden my sister's boyfriend and best friend are dating." I lifted my hands up, grimacing, "I don't know, do you see something wrong with that picture?"

"I think you are being extremely insensitive about this right now," Angela claimed her voice reaching a high octave of surprise. Angela stood up, her 5-foot frame leaning forward menacingly. "And I don't have to defend myself against your ridiculous accusations." She ripped at her purse that was at her side, as if trying to prove that her chihuahua-like anger was menacing.

"Really? I am?" I scoffed. "Bottom line, Angela, do what you want, but don't expect my approval." Bam, I said it, even though my heart was racing and my face was burning.

Angela stomped toward the door and put on her turquoise flats in a hasty rage that seemed out of character for her usual innocence. As if to make a point she slammed the door and I flinched.

~

It wasn't as if I had never planned to see Alana again. She was back and it was obvious the confrontation would come sooner or later, but when she appeared in my room, I could only leap a mile into the air because for some reason, the idea that my dead sister was hanging around was something I found a little hard to get used to.

"W-what are you doing here?" I stammered, electric shock

racing through my body.

Alana grinned, "It's my house too, is it not?"

I didn't answer, choking on the apple that was swelling in my throat.

"Or maybe it's not *really* my house anymore," Alana snorted, throwing her blonde hair over her shoulder, rage touching her light eyes. "I just don't get it. I don't know what went wrong. Or why the *hell* of all people," she looked at me, her eyes withholding so much pain, "*he* is with *her*." She grimaced with disgust and then spun around, pacing in the other direction.

Shrugging, I felt the intense nerves settle in my stomach. "It's not right," I said, coming to Alana's immediate defense.

She shot me a look. "Maybe I was a bad person while I was here. Maybe I aimed my hatred towards the wrong people." She blinked then averted her eyes, but I noticed the glint of a tear forming in her beautiful blue eyes. "I really am sorry," she managed, her voice cracking with the word 'sorry' - the word I never thought I would live to hear.

Holding my breath I looked away from her tall figure sauntering back and fourth in my room. "What do you mean?" I asked. But I knew what she meant. God, I knew what she meant. She was sorry for tormenting me, for ruining me. I didn't need to ask the question but it escaped my lips because part of me wanted her to explain why she was sorry, if she understood anything that she had done to me.

Alana turned to me, stopping dead in her tracks, "I think you know, Ivy," she said, tipping her head to the side. Of course I knew.

Dipping my gaze to the floor, I said nothing. There was nothing to say. I couldn't say it was alright because it wasn't.

I looked up when I felt Alana's hand cupped under my chin. Alana's blue eyes looked back at me, vacant, even though she was trying to hard to be sincere. Her eyes seemed to be brighter. Altered. Everything about her seemed to be different. "I really am sorry," she whispered.

The apple in my throat grew bigger as I shook my face from her grasp.

Without meaning to, my mind dove back into the past. I was a very sensitive person, it was a curse I was struggling to manage. As much as I tried to brush off what my sister had done to me and said to me, it didn't quite work that way. My self-esteem was never high enough to take what I did from my sister. When I was eight, she decided she wanted nothing to do with me anymore. After dealing with our parent's death, and the devastation that crashed us down as a family, we had moved out to Gran and grandpas.

The entire house felt like a reminder of the unfamiliar. It wasn't like we visited often enough to even feel comfortable. At eight, I remembered the transfer. That was when Alana started to close me off from her life. It started with little things, like her not wanting me to partake in her playing with Angela or anyone else that she brought over and it only grew to harassment. I didn't know how to stop it, so it only persisted.

Pretending it wasn't happening seemed to be the way I would cope. It was okay for me to be in the background. I could fade. I was alright with that because I never had to be in the light that Alana was in. I didn't have it. Slowly, I began closing myself off from my sister, avoiding her any time I could. There was no reason why it started. All I knew was the shame that came with it; my own sister didn't like me. My own family didn't want me.

Alana started with simple things like calling me ugly in front of her friends who would all laugh or I would hear her explain to her friends about how I was a reject and how Gran and grandpa took me in out of pity. Words really began to hurt at that age. That was when I started to lock myself in my room and read.

If there was any point in which I would be in the same location as Alana, I knew that she would say something that would degrade my self esteem in one way or another. It was exhausting to deal with, day in and day out. There was no escape.

Sometimes, I pretended to be the characters I read about, the strong ones, the determined ones, the funny ones, the ones who had something in them. They all had a light. They were all something special. I, on the other hand, had nothing special. I wasn't particularly smart or clever. I wasn't particularly pretty or outgoing. I was socially awkward and timid. There was nothing.

Escaping was easier than dealing with the fact that I was beginning to believe what I had been told my entire life.

Raising my eyes to Alana's bright blue eyes, I didn't say a word.

"I know you can't forgive me now, but I'm hoping that someday in the future you can," Alana said, whisking her blonde hair over her shoulder. Her apology was short-lived but there wasn't much else she could say without it actually being her. It was what I would get and I would have to accept that.

"We can move forward," I concluded, swinging my legs back and fourth on the bed. It was the best response I could give at the time. It wouldn't be good enough for Alana but it was all I could honestly give.

Alana didn't budge from her spot but finally nodded her head in understanding.

Robeline - Accusations

"And that was that?" Robeline asked, her dark eyes probing mine.

"And that was that," I agreed, my eyes falling to the floor. Examining the bottom corner of the wall, I noticed there were black scuffs around the off-white trimming, probably from Robeline sliding her chair back with force. I wondered if she had ever gotten angry with a patient before. Or vice versa. She didn't really look like she had it in her to get forcefully angry. But even I knew better than to judge a book by its cover.

Robeline sniffed, and I noticed with horror that she sounded stuffy. That was why the pungent smell of eucalyptus seemed to occupy the room. Leaning back, I looked at her with disgust.

"So you're sick." I winced out of repulse.

She looked up at me with blank shock, "It's the end of my cold, it's probably not contagious anymore."

"Thanks for your reassurance," I said, "just don't breathe on me."

Robeline seemed to

ignore my distain and continued. "When your sister apologized to you..." she paused, "Why did she do that after her death of all times?"

"Maybe she had time to reflect and realized she was a shitty person when she was alive, how should I know?" I snapped. "Why are you even questioning this?" I crossed my arms. "How should I know what she went through after dealing with her death?"

"Timing is important," Robeline stated, leaning forward. "All of these questions are essential to me understanding your story as well as your emotions," she murmured, a steely look in her eyes. I didn't want to question her work or what she did for a living but it seemed a little misconstrued. Sighing, my glance shot around the room. Hoping she would see my annoyance, I started to peel at my shoe again. *Click-tap-click-tap-click-tap.*

"Why did you accuse Angela of having something to do with Alana's disappearance?"

"Anger," I said, "It's not like it wasn't suspicious as it was, I just voiced it, that's all."

Robeline nodded, satisfied with my answer. "So you were mad at Angela because she was with Alana's boyfriend. Even though it had been three months," Robeline tilted her head, her eyes penetrating mine. "Do you think it could have been jealousy maybe?"

"Jealousy," I scoffed aloud and rolled my eyes. Needless to say, I was taken aback from her comment. "It's like you're not hearing me here," I complained. "I found it highly inappropriate for them to date while my sister was still missing."

"Yes, but you said yourself that your sister was dead and you knew this because of the ghost-like apparition that showed up as Alana. If Alana was dead, wasn't it only right for Matt and Angela to move on?"

"It was," I agreed, "If they knew she was dead but they didn't know and…" I lost my train of thought and looked down, frustration leaking through every atom of my body. "Maybe I was wrong, okay? Who cares?" Rolling my eyes, I examined the ceiling panels, trying to keep my frustration to a minimum. It didn't look good and it wasn't worth losing my cool over. Taking a deep breath, I tried to calm my frazzled nerve endings that were alight in my chest, threatening to burst.

"Why am I bothering you right now?" Robeline asked, narrowing her eyes in confusion.

"You're making me feel bad over something that I just find

inappropriate. I can't help that I do and I apologize that you just don't see things the way I do but I really don't think that makes me a bad person," I reasoned cautiously. "It feels like we're going over something over and over and over and it just seems like it's the wrong thing to go over. Who cares? I didn't find it appropriate. Sorry," I fell back against the chair, my arms crossed in defiance.

"I'm just trying to understand your train of thought," Robeline said. "Can I ask you a few more questions?" She asked.

"Yeah, whatever," I muttered.

"You went through various changes since your sister had gone missing. Suddenly you felt as though your clothes weren't good enough and your looks weren't good enough, why the sudden feeling of hatred toward your old life?" Robeline asked, her eyes scrutinizing me.

Shaking my head I tried to come up with the answer she wanted to hear. I didn't even know why I started changing so much. What did it matter? "I don't know," I shrugged, shaking my head. "I really don't. Maybe I've always felt that way… Maybe I decided I just wanted to be pretty for a change. Maybe I just felt like I had to live up to something for Gran and grandpa since Alana was gone. I really don't know."

"It sounds like you do," Robeline said more to herself then to me. "Please continue."

Alana – Fading away

I felt as though it was my right to stalk everyone who had moved on without me. It was my right to make sure they were okay. And they always were. I didn't know what hurt more, the fact that they all moved on or the fact that they were living as if I was never there.

Matt was happy. Angela was happy. Keith and Tanya were better considering I wasn't there to complicate things. Gran and grandpa would be fine without me, I knew it was just a matter of time before they moved on too. Of course they would take a bit more time. Overall, everyone was fine. Everyone except for me. I didn't know what was wrong with me, but I prayed that I would wake up from this goddamn nightmare.

I hoped that I wasn't dead. But I seemed to lose pieces of myself as time ticked on. It was unexplainable and a sure sign that I was running out of time or sanity, if that was even possible in my condition.

I seemed to forget simple things like the exact length of my hair or the way my hands looked. When that happened I found that my body would morph into whatever I thought I looked like. Funny thing is, I couldn't seem to remember. I would stare at my hands for longer than I would like to admit. Did they look different from everyone else's? Of course they did, but the way they used to look was blank in my mind now. My fingernails - Did I chew them off because I was nervous, or did I grow them out and paint them? I didn't seem to remember anything. What exact shade was my hair? And why did it feel like I was drifting in a dream-like state. It was more painful than any pain I had witnessed in my life...What did it feel like to be alive?

All I found myself doing was watching the people who used to be in my life. Hoping that I would find something of myself. The thing that I seemed to forget was that people evolve and change. The people I had once known and were close with weren't the same people anymore. I knew their names but I didn't know *them* anymore. Still, I followed them around, letting the fact that I was no longer a part of their lives hurt me over and over. That was the thing about my energy; it wouldn't die. I just didn't realize how torturous that would be.

I couldn't understand why I was still here, lingering in the in-between and suffering every second of my pathetic existence. It was time to move on, yet the only conclusion that I could come up with to save myself, was to fix what had gone wrong. I couldn't fix the obvious, however; the fact that I wasn't supposed to be dead because I was still very much alive. Still, I had to do something because I was turning into something I hated.

I found myself in a fit of jealousy due to the fact that everyone around me lived a life that they weren't scared to lose. Just like I did. But who lost that battle - me. It wasn't supposed to end like that. I had lived their oblivion before and it lead me to something worse than hell. Yet there they were, living, breathing, and making something of themselves. It was time for me to take circumstances into my own hands or drown in a sea of pity. And I've never been much for pity.

First thing that needed to be destroyed was Matt and Angela's relationship. I loved Angela, I wanted nothing more than for her to fall in love, but did it really have to be with *my* boyfriend? And Matt pretty much launched a sword through my torso and nailed me to the wall. Maybe I'm being melodramatic, but Matt wasn't supposed to be with Angela; he was supposed to be with me. That was obvious.

Stiffened up against the window, I watched as Angela leaned

over the counter in her washroom, smearing thick, white cream on her face, making her skin even more ghastly. Shocking. Snickering to myself, I turned and peered into her bedroom. The light pink walls struck a vivid memory.

Ivy and I were playing in the park when we met Angela. She was shy and timid, staring down at the ground and then back up at us as if signaling that she wanted to play. We were playing grounders and found it difficult with just the two of us. Somehow, Angela jumped in and started playing without communication of any sort. I guess that's the simplicity of being a kid. After that, we went back to Angela's house to play.

I knew Angela was going to be my best friend the moment she pulled out a VHS of Pokémon. We all sat down on the floor in front of the television, our legs crossed. It was our first real memory with Angela. And all of this rushed back to me because of the faint pink on the walls.

Lingering outside Angela's bedroom window, I watched as the light shut off in the bathroom. She had taken her makeup off and I couldn't help but tear apart her flaws. Her uneven skin tone seemed even more apparent in the yellow glare of her stained glass lamp. Why was Matt even with her? Angela paused and then turned around and walked out of the room. I squinted hard through the window, desperate she would come back soon. My patience was dwindling.

I gripped the knife I had found and carried with me. I don't know why I was so drawn to it, but I held it tight in my hand, the metal cool against my skin.

Angela came back a second later, a glass of water in hand. She sipped it and walked toward her bed. She set the glass down on the nightstand and fumbled with a hair band on her wrist. Winding it around her short hair, she placed it in a high ponytail at the top of her head. Not all of the hair made it into the ponytail, most of it made a short halo around her head. She didn't seem to care. She tossed back her sheets and slipped into bed, not even thinking twice. I almost felt bad. *Almost.*

Taking a deep breath, I waited, anticipating my moves. Time went by quickly. I stared at my own reflection in the glass. It wasn't long before the whole house went quiet and the lights shut off. I slipped into the night and moved to the back door, which was unlocked. It felt like it had been a decade since I had been in her house. I still felt it was good to be careful and diligent considering I had one goal in mind.

Creeping up the stairs, I started for her room. Everything

seemed to echo throughout the house, every step, every breath. It was a wonder how that was even possible or if it was just a figment of my imagination. My mind still thought there was some part of me that was alive. My mind expected to hear those sounds.

My heart pounded as my hand touched the doorknob of her room. My fingertips began to turn the knob. My blood coursed through my fingertips, again, my imagination. That hurt me even more because there was no blood to pulse through my body because I had no body. I was in limbo. I was pathetic. But I could change that. I had barely an ounce of power but I would use it to my best ability.

The door creaked open and my breath stilled in my throat. The anticipation of my goal made me giddy with excitement. The fact that she was my friend and she had trusted me was the only thing that was holding me back but I had to keep in mind that she wasn't the same person anymore. The real Angela would have never done anything to hurt me. In actuality, I would be helping get rid of her evil ways.

My eyes caught my reflection in the windowpane across from the door. The apparition of what I thought I would look like stared back at me, blue eyes bright. My hand was tight on the knife, numb with anticipation, but steady in my grasp.

The clicking of the vent seized. Everything in the room froze. The only sound was Angela's soft, shallow breathing. She could have fallen asleep pretty easily but I doubted it. Craning my head around the doorframe, I stared into the darkness. The bundle under the blankets moved, but hardly, it was more of a twitch.

My mind wandered back to seeing Angela and Matt together. I let it hurt me all over again. It took over every part of me. I had to think back to the pain otherwise I couldn't go through with doing what I was about to do. Even though I hated her with every part of me, it was hard to act on my impulses. I didn't know whether I could do it or not, but here I was, ready to attack. I was already in her goddamned room; there was no turning back now. It was too late. It was always too late. Regret hit every part of my body, making it ache.

I looked at myself in the black window again, my eyes tracing every feature. My body went limp instantly and the knife clanged to the floor, shattering the silence of the room.

Angela sat straight up in bed, her light eyes wide. I had managed to dive under her bed in that time.

Ivy – Losing control

Washing my hands, I glanced up at my eyes in the mirror. They were bloodshot and red. My reflection blinked at me as I continued to stare. Eyeliner was smeared on my left eye, my face was sunken as if I was deflating. It was never really easy to hide my emotions, they seemed to blow up all over my face and I couldn't seem to help it. The only thing that could possibility help was sleep.

It was time to try to go to bed and even the thought of it sickened me. Every time the sun went down, I wrestled with the question of whether or not I was going to sleep. All I wanted was a solid night of sleep, was that too much to ask? It felt like I was struggling with so much, with my lack of purpose, yet my biggest concern was not getting enough fucking sleep. It made me feel like there was something wrong with me. Was that even a question, of course there was. Normal people didn't feel the way I felt.

Tears sprang to my eyes and leaked down my face. I couldn't seem to bring my eyes back up into the mirror. I couldn't see myself lose control, even if I was alone.

I was embarrassed, but I couldn't hold it in. I was at war with myself, forcing the tears to stall for a moment, only for it to start again, harder this time. Alana had told me once that I was an ugly crier and although I had brushed it off like she was joking, I knew she wasn't. Then again, I'd love to meet the person who looks hot while a mess of fluid runs down their face.

It started off with tears springing to my eyes but turned into a heavy heaving. My back to the door in the washroom, I fumbled with the doorknob in attempt to lock the door. The last thing I wanted was for Gran to come and investigate. I knew grandpa wouldn't, he knew a little more about privacy.

I liked to blame my tears on lack of sleep. I was exhausted beyond comprehension and the side effects of it were even worse. It felt like I was losing my mind. I would hallucinate and my words would jumble together. I was pumped full of adrenalin for no reason at all. It felt as if everything wrong that could happen in my life was happening. It started with crying over lack of sleep. It turned into crying over my life.

Every aspect of my life was a mess; nothing turned out right. I wasn't the person I wanted to be and crying about it had an awful way of dragging me deeper and deeper into a pit of self-pity. I was good at hiding my emotions and keeping them bottled up. I *was*. That was the last thing that I could identify with myself. I could bottle up my emotions, that's it. Even that turned out to be false. However, the release of my emotions felt good and once I started, I to let go.

I thought about my sister and her sudden disappearance. Then I thought about how I couldn't sleep and how I had no idea what I was doing and how everyone in my life expected better from me, including myself. In that, I felt helpless. My dead sister who had traumatized me as a child was haunting me and now that she was gone, I was open to the idea of actually accepting the fact that she really hurt me because in her absence everything was better. *Everything.* How do you even explain that?

The only thing I could think of that could possibly make me feel better was to have a drink or ten, something to numb my feelings that were taking over. I couldn't handle it anymore. So it was true that we all turn to something to seize the pain. I was lying to myself if I couldn't admit that everything in my life was on a downward spiral.

I had lied to myself for so long that when the realization hit me, it hit harder than ever.

When I looked up into the mirror, my hollow dark eyes stared back at me. That's when I noticed the blonde hair behind my head in the corner of the mirror. Shocked, I spun around. Alana had appeared behind me.

"What are you so upset about?" Alana murmured, lifting her hand up to stroke my hair.

Recoiling, I spun away from her, my lower back hitting the sink with a loud thump. My face burned with embarrassment.

Gran's slippers padded toward the closed bathroom door that I stood behind. My breath stilled in my throat, I was still petrified at my sister's sudden appearance. Gran hesitated in front of the door before she knocked. "Ivy?" She asked, her voice shrill with confusion.

"Y-yes?" I stammered, my eyes glued on Alana's piercing blue eyes.

"Is everything alright in there?" Gran asked.

Alana raised her eyebrows and I glared back at her.

"Yes, everything's fine," I said automatically, "Just dropped something."

There was an eerie silence at the door as Gran contemplated leaving.

Clenching my hands into fists, I noticed the dewy sweat that had formed on my hands the second Alana had arrived. My hand twitched as I waited for Gran to leave, every second seeming like a full minute.

"Alright then… good night," Gran said, speculation hanging in her voice.

I waited for Gran steps to fade away before I spoke.

"What are you doing here?" I snapped, glaring at Alana. My voice was louder than I intended it to be and I cringed, hoping Gran wouldn't turn around and come back.

Spinning toward the door I pressed my hands up against it and peered out the crack between the door and the doorframe but I couldn't see anything. I didn't even know why I bothered.

"I came to check on you, little sis," Alana grinned as she moved towards the sink and jumped up on it. "It looks like you aren't doing so well," she claimed, looking me over from a higher level. "It's clear you're stressed about something." She barked a laugh and then choked on it in surprise, as she looked me over.

"Are those my clothes?" Alana asked, blinking in shock, her eyes looking me up and down in scrutiny.

Looking down, I noticed the floral pattern on the tank top

that I had stolen. Maybe not really a necessity but it looked nice. I had dug through her drawers and taken some of her clothes, only the ones that looked good on me, which was almost all of them. They were flattering on me. I wasn't swimming in fabric, which was something new. My old clothes seemed to do nothing with my figure like Alana's did.

"Uh..." I had meant to tell Alana about this but I forgot how abrupt she could be.

Alana kinked her head to the side, her eyes narrowed. "Why in the hell did you steal my fucking clothes?" she demanded, her eyes lighting up with resentment.

"It's not like you can even wear them anymore!"

Alana blinked at me, at a loss for words. It was obvious she was taken a back by my choice of words. "Yeah, I guess." She looked down at her hands. The look in her eyes pulled at my heart and I immediately felt bad for letting my tongue slip. It was something that was happening far too frequently.

"I didn't mean that," I said immediately. It was too late; I couldn't take it back.

Seconds ticked by and finally Alana shrugged, "Yeah you did. It's fine. It's nothing compared to the shit I put you through. I guess I'm not really here and I don't know why it makes me mad," she paused, cocking her head to the side. "For the record, you look good. Other than the tears, obviously."

Putting her words together, I cocked my head to the side. There was no way my sister was actually complimenting me and meaning it. That wasn't her.

"What do you want, Alana?" I demanded, my frustration obvious. Brushing my palms against my eyes, I tried to wipe every last tear from my face.

"Tell me what's bothering you," Alana murmured, her glassy eyes looking me over.

"Why do you care?" I snapped. "You wouldn't get anything out of it."

"What's that supposed to mean?" Alana snarled, taken aback.

"It's supposed to mean you're selfish."

"As are you," Alana threw back at me, folding her arms across her chest. "It's human nature."

"But you don't try to combat it, or stop it."

"Why would I bother?"

I didn't have an answer for that so instead I just stared at her, letting the silence sink in. "I just don't want to be fucked up."

Alana barked a laugh and combed her fingers through her platinum hair. "That's what you're concerned about?"

"What?" I snapped, irritated. "Why can't that bother me? I mean I have every right to feel scared about where my life is going, I haven't been sleeping, I don't have friends. I don't have a boyfriend... I'll probably end up alone. In fact, I don't see myself ever moving out of this house," the truth of my words was starting to sink in, it made me want to choke up all over again. Instead, I swallowed the apple growing in my throat.

Alana looked exhausted with my explanation. Her head was cocked to the side; her eyes squinted at me, scrutinizing my words. I took a deep breath and continued, "I'm tired of not being liked... I'm tired of being me... of being screwed up."

"So what are you going to do about it? Is this the start of you changing yourself to match what you think if normal?" She paused and shook her head, a scowl on her face. "Since when did any of this bother you?"

"Since now!" I paused and tried to gather my emotions. "I just want to be normal. I don't want to end up fucked up."

"See, that's the thing that you don't realize," Alana laughed, pushing herself off of the counter and onto the floor. She spun around and started to fluff her hair in the mirror.

I sighed, immediately irritated by her response. "What don't I realize, Alana?"

Alana smirked back at me in the mirror. "We're all a little fucked up."

Her words echoed through my head. I forced a laugh. "Yeah, whatever Alana. When have you ever been 'fucked up?'"

Alana's face changed then. She shook her head, a mess of blonde hair falling around her shoulders. "I'm not feeling okay, Ivy. I'm scared." She looked up at me. "I've never been so afraid."

Blinking in confusion, I folded my arms. Her emotions were changing so fast. This didn't seem like her. Something was wrong. "Why are you so afraid, Alana? What happened?"

Alana clicked her tongue and dipped her gaze down to her hands. "It feels like I don't even know what I'm doing anymore," she murmured, "It started with small things, like forgetting simple aspects about myself and it turned into…" she shook her head as if realizing she had no idea what she was trying to say.

Sighing, she continued, "I don't know what I'm doing

anymore, I really don't."

Narrowing my eyes the question escaped my lips, "What happened?"

Alana – I was never your friend

My breathing was shallow and quiet. Parallel to the sudden movement in Angela's room. The eerie glow of her stain glass lamp threw soft shades of blue, purple and pink all over the room.

Angela climbed out of bed and I watched from beneath her bed as she put on her ugly pink slippers that she kept tucked slightly beneath the bed. She padded around to her door and stared in silence, as if confused. She was wondering where the clash of my knife hitting the floor came from.

I had scooped up the knife and dove under the bed before she had seen me. If she would have, that is. It was a wonder why I was still hiding. It was probably because I was scared to make a move. Part of me loved Angela, I really did. I had known her for too long to make a move but I anticipated it. I just needed time to pull myself together.

I was running out of time, I had to do what I had come for. Taking a deep breath, I rolled out from underneath the bed and faced Angela head on, the knife hot in   my hand.

A look of confusion crossed her face. Seeing the knife, she backed up against the window, her hands up by her face. "What are you doing here?" She shrieked. "Did you sneak in?"

Shocked that she could see me I couldn't find the words to say. "Oh," I muttered, falling back in shock.

Angela glared at me, "What are you doing here?" She asked, her voice shrill. "What are you doing in my room?" She demanded, her voice getting louder and louder.

It was like she didn't see the knife. Or didn't believe I was an actual threat, because I was *pathetic* lately.

"Why are *you* screaming at *me* like that?" I demanded anger flooring through my body. "You've changed into somebody I don't even know. It's like you don't even care about how I feel! Why am I not even a memory to you?" I shook my head and stepped away from her, caught up in emotions that fogged my brain.

Angela stared at me in silence, her eyes drawing towards the door every few seconds. I could see the gears turning in her head but Angela was too uncoordinated to actually get away.

"Why are you doing this?" Angela asked me, her voice shaking in tremors, she arched her back and walked backwards to the nearest wall, cornering herself like a lost sheep.

"I think you know the answer to that question," I murmured, pressing the tip of blade to my lip and looking up in exaggerated thought. My mind wandered back to the memory of Angela at Matt. It was what fuelled me. "Angela, you were supposed to be my friend, don't you feel bad at all?" I asked, shaking my head and bringing the knife back down in front of me.

"I was never your friend," Angela whispered, her voice shaking.

It was as though a hot knife had seared through my body. Holding my breath, I tried to calm my emotions that were whirling at that moment. It was as if she punched me in the chest. I swung the knife back.

"Well," I forced a grin, "I guess that makes this a little less tragic."

Ivy - Gone

Placing my books into the cardboard box, I held my breath simultaneously. I didn't know what I was doing or why. My books weren't serving me much purpose. I had stopped reading. Having books that I had read over and over seemed senseless anyway. I could recite some of them by heart.

They all reminded me of Alana, each and every single one of them. Piling them one on top of another in a stack, memories flooded back to me. It would happen one last time before I would donate them and I would never have to see them again. Most of the books were from Alana. They were from Christmas or my birthday. She would give me a book every year as if it were a tradition. For that one day she was always nice to me. Maybe it was because it was a holiday and it was hard for anyone to be mad, but it made holidays easier. Of course, she would always go back to treating me like crap afterwards. Not having to pretend that it wasn't happening for that one day was nice for a change.

Smiling at the memory,

I looked at the books one by one, remembering the storyline of each one. The bright covers reminded me of my boring past. Reading was an obsession of mine; it was nice to escape my life and pretend I was someone else, in a different place, with different problems. That escape was relieving. After a couple days, I would be on a search to find the next book to dive into. I was always happy when I was deep in a good book. Anything to take me away.

Frowning, I uncovered some of the more recent books she had given me. Tears started to prick at my eyes but I held my breath and scooped the remainders up, dropping them into the box. "Fuck you," I muttered, staring down at the box. And screw you for leaving me, I thought, tears stinging my eyes now. I was only left with remnants of Alana's life, reminders that I would be better off without.

The doorbell interrupted my thoughts and I stood up, alarmed. Wiping at my eyes, I started toward the door of my room that was wide open. Gran had already got the door. She was murmuring quietly to someone. She stepped back, looking over at me, her eyes wide.

"Ivy?" she called. Her eyes locked with mine and she gave me a puzzled look as if asking what I was doing standing there like an idiot, either that or questioning the box beside my bookshelf.

Shaky, I started out my room and towards the door.

Gran turned and walked toward the kitchen, but I could tell she was planning on eavesdropping by her lingering stare.

Craning my head around, I peered toward the door and my eyes locked on Tanya's dark stare. Blinking with shock, I half-jogged to the door. "Hi?" I questioned, my voice shrill and distant. Clearing my throat, I narrowed my eyes at Tanya. Her makeup was absent. I noted the hair obscuring her dark eyes that were red rimmed and darting away every few seconds. Something wasn't right.

"What are you doing here?" I asked.

"I-uh," Tanya looked down at her hands. A long strand of dark hair fell over her face and she shook her head. "Angela's gone."

Frozen in place, I stared at Tanya. It was the first time I had seen her remorseful over something that didn't involve her. Part of me found it hard to believe. There was no way Tanya actually had a soul. Her words seemed hollow and fake. It was almost as if I hadn't heard her properly.

"W-what do you mean 'gone'?" I stuttered.

Tanya rolled her eyes and stepped backward on the concrete stairs, "Angela's dead," she choked, her voice trembling.

I opened my mouth to reply, but I had no words. Instead, I

rambled, "I just saw her the other day…"

Tanya sighed and shifted her weight, impatient with my answer. "She was murdered last night." She rolled her eyes, as if I forced her to say it.

Time seemed to stop. Tanya stood awkwardly on the step for a second longer before spinning around and running down the steps, yanking at her black sleeves and wiping them across her eyes. She jumped into Keith's car. They sat there a second before roaring off and leaving me in shock.

The word 'murdered' echoed through my mind. It didn't seem to register.

Ivy – The funeral

Matt stared into his hands, his eyes heavy. Twice in a row this had happened to him and I couldn't help but feel sorry for him. But I also felt suspicious. I tried to hold back and mask it, after all, it was Matt; he had been a part of my life for so long. However, it seemed like too many unexplainable things had happened and I couldn't help but question the occurrences in our small town.

Inconspicuous stares magnetized towards Matt. Some were pity, but most held a touch of blame. Twice his girlfriend died; double the suspicion. In a small town, a rep like that wouldn't ever disappear.

The energy in the church was heavy. One by one, people who were friends with Angela or involved with her in some way, poured in and took seats. Angela's parents sat at the front, her mother weeping loudly, her back hunched with racking sobs. Her father, tears in his eyes, rubbed her mother's back in attempt to comfort her.

Staring down at my

black dress, I knocked my shoes together and examined my feet. The sole near my heel was beginning to fray on my left foot. Trying to hold my distraction, I picked at it with my right foot.

I didn't know Angela very well but she was my sister's best friend. That was enough to make me uncomfortable. The emotions in the church made me want to hold my breath. I didn't feel comfortable there with everyone weepy. It almost made me teary-eyed.

The wooden backing of the long bench I was sitting on was beginning to hurt my back. The lip of the seat dug into my upper back. Uncomfortable, I shifted. Taking a glance toward Matt, I saw him stand up. *Oh no,* I thought internally. He was going to say a speech.

Cringing, I watched as he walked to the front. Every sound in the church seemed to stop in an instant. He took the mic at the front. Gritting my teeth, I stared hard at my shoes. Every eye seemed to be on him. He cleared his throat and fumbled with the Q-cards in his shaky hands.

"A-Angela was a bright soul," he paused and blinked away tears. He took a deep breath and continued. "She was full of life and beauty. She inspired me by the way she looked at life. She would find the good in anything and anyone. She was my flame; a light in a dreary situation. She always held her head high with determination that I had never known in a person until her," he stopped, holding his breath as if scared to cry. I couldn't help but wonder, *what about my sister? She was full of life too… She held an even brighter light.* **You destroyed that.** Alarmed and embarrassed at my accusing thought, I quickly looked back down at my lap. I had nothing against Matt and no reason to be skeptical of him other than the idea that twice in a row something awful and suspicious happened. It was not enough of a reason for me to accuse him of the death of two women.

Twisting uncomfortably in my seat, I caught sight of Tanya toward the back of the church as Matt's speech droned on. Tanya was staring toward the front, unblinking. She caught my glance and scowled. Shocked, I quickly turned back around.

It was only then, that I began to realize how suspicious it was that Tanya told me she thought Alana should just die the night Alana went missing. Curious, I began to wonder if maybe there was more to the story than I had originally thought. I did know that Alana was cheating on Matt with Keith. Maybe I shouldn't feel bad for accusing people of the death of my sister. It was reasonable, considering there was a murderer out there. Maybe it wasn't so wrong for me to look for my sister's killer. But then again, it really could have been anyone. It even could have been Angela.

Breaking away from my thoughts, I returned to the ending of Matt's speech. "I will never know why you were taken so early on," he managed, "I-I will miss you forever, Angela. You will always be in my heart," he choked tears at the end of his speech. Everyone seemed to think it was genuine, crying in unison with him. I couldn't help but question his sincerity.

The pallbearers all took a place around Angela's coffin. I wondered how bad the murder was. We emerged into the cool fall air and toward the burial. The cold air bit my neck; I covered up my bare skin with my long trench coat.

Tanya, dressed in a navy dress, made her way over to Matt and placed her hand on his lower back as they entered the cool air. She seemed as though she was trying to comfort him.

Shooting my glance back I caught a look of disdain crossing Keith's face.

~

Walking through the door of the drugstore, a bell clanged through the air, making me leap with shock. I was tense after leaving Angela's funeral. I had one goal coming in here, shampoo. I strolled directly toward the hair aisle. The heel of my shoe seemed to smack against the floor as I walked. Frustrated, I peered down only to notice the skeleton of my shoe peering out from the sole. Groaning in anger, I stuffed it back into the fabric, knowing it would only pop out again.

We had ripped through the value-sized shampoo faster than normal, which was weird because Alana wasn't even using it anymore. It could have been an over use of shampoo in my hair which was sadly leaving it dull and lifeless. The smell also seemed to nauseate me like it never had before. Watermelon-cucumber. I used to love it. It used to smell fresh and summery.

It was obvious I needed something new. Something that didn't make me want to hurl while I was taking a shower. Examining the shampoo bottles, I looked for different scents. I could do a change to hibiscus flowers. That was always pretty. I grabbed a bottle of shampoo. The bottle of conditioner was right beside it. Staring at it blankly, I grabbed it as well. There was no sense lying to myself, I hated the scent of the conditioner too. It smelled like Alana.

Content with my decision, as I left the isle, something caught my eye. It was boxed dye. I stared at it blankly. Bottle blonde. Alana always got her hair done at the salon. I was too cheap for a salon, but

I did question the color. Looking into the little mirror that was attached to a flap labeled lipstick on the other side, I noticed my light skin tone. It occurred to me that I could pull it off. But I would look a lot like Alana, especially if I straightened my hair and let it grow out a little more. Stretching my wound up, mousy curl from the back of my neck, it reached just above my breast. It would look good. But what would everyone else think?

Was it too soon to dye my hair after my sister had gone missing? I wondered if people would question it. It would still look good.

On impulse, I grabbed the box and started for the register.

The cashier was turned around but the light was on so I dropped all of my stuff on the counter and I smiled when she looked at me, an attempt to be somewhat friendly.

The cashier forced a smile that looked more like a grimace and started ringing through the shampoo and hair dye. Her hand fell upon the box of dye and she looked up at me. I noticed that she was from school. She was one of my 'friends' from high school. She flipped the box over and then looked up at me and scowled. I could already see what she was thinking.

She thought I was trying to turn into Alana. It was distasteful because Alana was gone yet here I was, buying dye that would make my hair vaguely the same color that Alana's used to be. Under her scrutiny, I began to feel nervous about wearing makeup and my clothes that weren't mine anymore. It was as if she could see what I was thinking, she examined me.

"On debit," I muttered, glaring at her.

~

Rising up from the sink, I looked into my mud brown eyes in the mirror. I wrapped the pink towel around my head and stared into my reflection. I hoped it would turn out good. My eyes fell to the model on the box smiling, her blond hair flying in mid air like some sort of force was holding it up. She was posing in the most unnatural pose. It was a wonder why people thought something so unnatural was attractive. I guess I just thought differently.

Yanking the towel off of my head, I stared into the mirror, anxious. My wet hair fell in dark blond clumps at the side of my face. Brushing it out, I watched in growing anticipation, waiting for it to dry. Watching it seemed to slow the process so I opened the bathroom door to leave.

Gran was walking by with a laundry basket but she stopped dead in her tracks at the sight of me. "What did you do?" She asked, looking behind me at the box on the counter.

"Relax," I muttered, combing out my hair with my fingers, "I just wanted a change."

Gran didn't respond, she just stared at me, as if waiting for another explanation.

"Doesn't it look good?" I asked, hoping for a compliment, something to make me feel like I didn't just wreck my hair.

"I'm sure it will look fine," Gran murmured, her eyes lingering on me before she turned around and went to my room to collect clothes that I had left on top of the laundry hamper for her.

Turning around, I grinned at myself in the mirror. My hair was drying quickly and the more it dried, the better it looked.

I realized with a burst of confidence, that it was my best transformation yet. I looked, pardon me if I boast, but I looked *stunning*. The color fit my skin tone perfectly. With my makeup and my new striking blond hair, I felt empowered. There was no trace of the old Ivy left. I had completely transformed and did it ever feel good!

My hair was beginning to dry and bounce up into the springy curls that I had before. Reaching for Alana's straightener, I tapped my left index finger on the ceramic plate. It seared my finger. Putting the straighter up to the top layer of my curls, I pulled it down, revealing the perfect, smooth blond hair that I had dreamed of.

The smoke from the straightener rose up into the air and all I could smell was the scent of my new shampoo, hibiscus flowers. The scent was so perfect. The look was perfect, and for once, I was perfect.

Robeline – Fulfillment

"So you finally felt complete," Robeline said, "And it's safe to say that you really hit a milestone with that because you have never really felt good about yourself."

Nodding I fell back into the chair, "Yeah I guess that sums it up. It finally felt like I was becoming who I was supposed to be, who I was *meant* to be," I sighed, looking past Robeline and at the walls behind her. "And at a time when I felt so desperate and lost because I had no idea who I was or what I wanted to do with my life. You can probably understand my relief," I laughed but the humor hardly radiated past me.

Robeline hardly twitched at my statement. I had opened up and made myself look awful, considering the fact that my transformation towards fulfillment happened after my sister had left my life. Finally, Robeline lowered her pen to her notepad and scribbled feverishly, pausing only to look at me and then back down, the flow of her pen not stopping.

My eyes fell to the

floor, going over the last thing that I had said.

"Angela's death," Robeline's voice cut through my mind with those words. "Can you tell me feelings that are associated with that?"

Heat flushed to my face. Keeping my head down, I started, "Well obviously it was upsetting, I mean I did just have a huge fight with her and then all of the sudden she dies." I shrugged, "How do you think that would make me feel?"

"Guilty?" Robeline asked, tilting her head.

"I guess," I said, rubbing my sweaty palms on my pants.

Robeline nodded, and then reached for the coffee on the table. It was Starbucks. I couldn't help but wonder what exactly it was. It was probably black coffee; bitter and bland to match her personality. But potent because she seemed to poke and prod at every useless detail.

"When Alana flat out admits to you that she had done something wrong and then you hear the news of Angela's death, why didn't you connect the two? Why didn't you even think of her as a suspect?" Robeline asked, as she took a sip of her coffee.

Narrowing my eyes, I thought back to that night. Robeline placed her cup down, still waiting for an answer. Yet, the only thing

I could think of was the fact that she believed me when I told her Alana was back. I guess it didn't really matter whether she believed me or not. The idea of it alone was far out. I just didn't like feeling like I was crazy. It was a feeling that I had far too often.

"She's my sister and I guess I didn't want to believe it," I murmured, blinking at the realization. "You only see what you want to, right? Besides, who wants to believe that their sister has gone crazy? Or maybe part of me just didn't want to believe it." It wasn't like she outright said it either. Pardon me for thinking my sister was better than that. Annoyed, I flicked my hair over my shoulder.

"But you already knew subconsciously," Robeline commented, her thin eyebrows flicking up.

Taken aback, I scowled at her in anger. Again, Robeline had proved herself to be unprofessional, but in a subtle way so I couldn't say anything. Not that I would.

"I'm just shocked that you didn't think of her as a suspect," Robeline shrugged. "Moving on," she looked up at me, expecting more.

Ivy – The car crash

Sitting down at the table, I avoided grandpa's stare that was burning into the back of my head from his chair in the living room. Crossing my legs underneath the table, I grasped the cutlery that Gran had put out for dinner. Gran still wasn't anywhere in sight, however, which was odd for her. She was usually putting the final touches on a meal and cleaning up the mess that she had started. She was neat and orderly, with everything in its place, she had been like that for years.

The creak of the recliner sliding back made me sit up straighter in my seat. Grandpa strode past my back, the air of him whooshing past me. Sighing, my eyes darted around the kitchen.

Finally grandpa spoke up after grunting. "Why the change in hair color?" he asked after what felt like forever. He scooped up his plate from his seat and walked toward the stove. Without hesitating, he piled two pork chops onto his plate and then stared at the rice, as if contemplating his options. He knew that Gran was one to take offense if he didn't eat a little bit of everything but grandpa was more of a meat kind of guy. He was fully fuelled by protein and the risk for high cholesterol. He would be screwed if he were a bachelor.

"It was time," I said, fiddling with the cutlery in my hands. That and Alana wasn't around to hound me about trying to look decent. I would have "copied" her. But in reality, it just looked good on me and I couldn't help that. My natural hair color was awful, I just didn't have the nerve to change it. Not while I was going to be harassed about it at least.

Grandpa walked past me again and took a seat at the head of the table, grunting in appreciation for his two pork-chop meal. He had taken a tablespoon of rice as if to say that he was arguably trying to be healthy. Gran would question him as soon as she walked in. Finally, he spoke, "It's funny, you look like her," grandpa admitted, his face falling at the thought. I didn't have to question who he was talking about.

"She would have thought I 'copied' her," I scoffed, finally standing up with my plate, giving up on waiting for Gran as well as grandpa did.

Grandpa laughed, shaking his head. "No, like Sharon, your mother. I suppose Alana looked like her as well." Grandpa shrugged, tears glistening in his eyes. Immediately, he shifted his gaze as if

166

pretending that the tears weren't there. He wasn't going to cry in front of me and part of me was thankful for that. I wouldn't know what to do if he had broken down. I hardly knew what to do when Gran cried in front of me.

Biting my lower lip I shrugged. "I didn't know her," I admitted in a whisper. "I guess I was too young." An apple began to swell in my throat. Swallowing, I forced it down and then cleared my throat. It wasn't worth getting upset about. I didn't even remember her or my father.

Grandpa smiled as if recalling a memory. He then shook his head. "That very well might have been. It's too bad. Your mother was an incredible women."

"She must have been," I said, "Alana was torn up about her and dad," I paused, "After it happened. Obviously I don't remember a thing." Bitterness leaked into my tone before I could stop it.

"It must have been more traumatic for you than you think," Grandpa stated, his eyes baring into mine. "You loved your parents more than you seem to remember. It was hard for you too. We had to put you through counseling," Grandpa shook his head. "I guess it didn't really work if you don't remember a thing. Or it did, depending on how you look at it," he said, shrugging.

Narrowing my eyes, I leaned forward. "What do you mean? Why did you and Gran put me through counseling?" I demanded, suddenly curious.

"You were in the car," Grandpa shook his head, narrowing his eyes at me, "don't you remember? You were eight. The car rolled on the way to your gymnastics class. Alana stayed here with us. The roads were miserable that day and your class was being hosted in Revelstoke, about an hour away from here. I guess it was bad timing considering the weather." Grandpa shrugged then dug into his pork chop.

My eyes remained glued to him chewing the dry pork chop, my mouth slightly agape. It was as if his words sent me flying back into the past, rehashing my blocked memory of the incident. And in a moment, I was swimming through my vivid past, reliving it.

I remembered now. I remembered my mother's blond hair in the passenger seat and how she had turned around to smile at me. She asked me 'Are you excited for your class, honey?' I nodded. My father was in the drivers seat. I could picture his short brown hair, his glasses mirroring his focused brown eyes glued to the road. His mouth was pressed into a line. My mother was trying to distract me from my fathers' quiet cursing as he squinted through the windshield. The snowplows still hadn't gotten to scraping the first layer of snow off of the road. It was early winter and the roads were icy; the lines weren't visible. As we travelled uphill, I noticed the yellow line. My dad was in the middle of the road. He didn't notice because he couldn't see. There was someone else coming over the hill and once he realized that, he swerved, pitching the car to the right. Too far right.

I remembered the silence as we flew into the air, the car tilting hard. The impact of the car hitting the ground forced all the air out of my lungs. My heart was beating so fast and so hard against my small ribcage, it hurt. And then over the car went again and again. The hollow sound of cracking glass was sickening, it rolled all the way up my spine as if to remind me that it was real. It was all real. All I could see when I opened my eyes was the smudged red blood in the cracks on the windows. All I could hear was my own ragged breath that progressed into high-pitched, gasping crying.

Holding my breath, I looked up as Gran entered the room. The memory was still fresh in my mind, haunting me. The disturbed cry of my eight-year-old self rang through my head.

"Excuse me," I managed, placing my plate back down on the table. Avoiding eye contact, I shuffled from behind the table. I could feel their burning stare, taking in every emotion that was likely plastered all over my face. The chair wobbled as I brushed past it, knocking it almost on its side. I caught it in haste and straightened it before rushing toward my room. It was like I was floating, moving at a quick pace to my room, where I may or may not feel safe. But it was better to break down without causing a scene, just another thing for my grandparents to worry about.

Closing the door behind me, I took a deep breath and held it. My eyes flickered up, reviewing my sanctuary.

"So I guess you know why I blamed you," Alana's soft voice tore through my already turbulent thoughts. "Part of me blamed you for their death. That maybe if you didn't have to go to your gymnastics thing, maybe they would still be alive. I know that's ridiculous. I just wanted them to be alive. I felt robbed... Everything would be different if they were still here, you know, maybe I wouldn't be dead. Maybe things could have turned out the way they should have."

My breath stilled in my throat. Staring at Alana, I looked her over, her clothes that she had died in and her perfectly colored hair. It was a shade lighter than mine.

"What do you want?" I demanded in a harsher tone than I

had expected.

Alana's eyes flared for a moment and she cocked her head to the side, as if holding back her irritation. "I want," she said loud and deliberate, "to *talk* to you."

"You had all of our lives to talk! Why now? Don't you think it's a little late? Anytime I ever wanted to talk to you when you were alive, I was pestering you - you just wanted me out of your life. You got your wish. Now just leave me alone!" I snapped, anger cutting off my airway.

Alana didn't move. My words didn't phase her. Her strength irritated me even more.

"I can't pretend what I did wasn't wrong and since you're the only one that can see me," Alana's voice rattled from emotion, "I figure I can, at least, try to repair things with you."

"It's too late," I said, shaking my head. "I spent years blaming myself. And then you come back here and think an *apology* will take all of those years of being treated like absolute shit away. Are you kidding me? You harassed me for something I couldn't help!"

"Try to understand it from my point of view, I was young and I knew it wasn't right to blame you for it but subconsciously, I did and I am sorry for that," Alana's stare bore into me as if to say, *why don't you just fucking get over it.* She was ignorant, she always was.

"I was eight!" I yelled suddenly, my voice ringing harshly throughout the room. Tears began to form in my eyes. Blinking them away, I collapsed onto my bed.

Silence. It was the response I wanted. Just for Alana to shut up and think. Alana sat beside me, swinging her feet back and fourth on the bed. Her stilettos shone in the light of my room. I found it hard to believe that she was actually dead and that her ghost form could mirror such an amazing image. It was all I could think about.

"Say something," I murmured.

Alana took in a deep breath, as if my permission was what she was waiting for. "Please, you're all I have now, Ivy. Nobody can see me and I can't apologize to people because they won't hear me. Try to understand how frustrating that is. I just want you to forgive me, but I guess I can understand if that is too much to ask."

No, she really didn't understand that that was too much to ask. I pressed my lips together, fighting back to urge to just let her have it. The urge slipped away as time ticked by.

Laying back onto the bed, I focused on the sounds of the

house. It all seemed to be so much louder in the sudden stillness. Alana fell back onto the bed beside me.

"I forgive you," I muttered. It was a lie that I was forced into. Alana wasn't going to take it very well if I didn't forgive her. I already knew that. "But I don't forgive you for murdering Angela," I said, sick with the thought.

Silence enveloped the room.

Alana didn't move. Finally, she turned to me, "I didn't kill Angela."

Ivy – To be that girl

Walking down the street, I yanked on my dark-wash jean shorts that were riding up high on my thighs. I wasn't used to wearing such provocative clothes but I was trying to get used to it. After all, wearing jeans all the time was boring and hot in the summer. It was one of the first few times I had worn shorts outdoors and I felt exposed in them. When people gawked, I thought it was because I looked ridiculous. Everyone wore shorts, I was just never that girl. Until now.

To say I didn't like the looks of surprise was a lie. I had nice legs and it was nice to finally feel comfortable in my skin and stop suffocating in oversized clothing that served me no other purpose than making me fade into the background. It was nice to be seen for a change. Even my walk was more confident.

I had decided to confront Matt for several reasons. Number one, if Alana didn't kill Angela, then who did? There was a killer out there, maybe the same killer who had killed my sister and I was tired of sitting back and doing nothing about it. The scariest part was the fact that the killer could be anyone I knew. It was time for me to start getting information. And I would have to do anything I could to get it.

Walking up the walkway to Matt's house, I fumbled with the doorbell. Was I supposed to ring it or knock? Why was this even a question? Embarrassed by my thought, I pressed my left index finger into the doorbell and fiddled with my hands, trying to sidetrack my nerves. Flicking my newly blond hair over my shoulder, I tried to gather every ounce of confidence that I had.

Then it hit me. What if one of his roommates opened the door? My heart leaped in my chest, and I spun around, surveying the street. The old me would have probably started running by now. Still, something kept me from moving. I was paralyzed in place.

I was tired of acting like an idiot. I was tired of the awkward situations I would bring into my life just by being an introvert who made a fool of myself in any social situation I was present in.

I gulped a breath of fresh air. I told myself I was someone else because being myself just wasn't an option anymore.

The door opened with a loud creek and I almost instantly felt like leaping into the bushes beside the door, hoping not to be seen or heard.

It was Matt. His hair was messy and obscuring his vacant, sad eyes. It was clear that Angela's death was still taking a huge toll on him. His eyes were glassy but widened at the sight of me. I was relived to see him.

"Ivy, wow," Matt stammered, blinking. He overlooked my appearance, as if in shock.

My hand fell to my left shoulder, gripping the black spaghetti strap, I twisted it, nerves whirling in my stomach. "Sorry if I shocked you," I said, glancing into his house. "Mind if I come in?" I asked.

Matt stepped aside as if I had ordered him. He gawked at me, seeming to be at a loss for words. I could feel his eyes burning into me, looking me over. Although it made me uncomfortable, it also felt good to finally be looked at like that. I was conflicted on whether to smack him or just take it as a compliment. I used to hate when men would look over women like a piece of meat. Now I was that piece of meat. Wincing, I dropped the thought and started to slide out of my shoes.

Smiling a tense and awkward smile, I walked into his house, stopping at the entrance to the kitchen. "Are you home alone?" I asked, before letting out a giggle of embarrassment at the question.

"I am," he said.

Looking down at my bare feet I hid my face. "I just can't be alone right now," I said, raising my eyes to him. "There's a murderer out there and-"

Matt dropped his gaze at that, staring at his feet. He was likely remembering Angela. Or Alana. Any of which could have hurt him by me rehashing the talk. Of course it was too early to talk about it.

"Well, I'm scared," I shrugged, and then let out a tense laugh that was likely out of place.

"Everyone is," Matt said. "Especially with… Angela." His eyes stared into mine.

Gridding my teeth, I nodded. "Yeah, pretty scary."

"Why did you dye your hair blonde?" Matt asked abruptly, as if he was aching to ask the question.

Combing my fingers through my hair, I smiled. "I think it suits me, don't you?" I asked. "Plus it's summer, it's always nice to lighten up." I wondered just how long I would have that question thrown at me. It wasn't enough that I looked better.

"It's funny, I didn't see the resemblance till now," Matt said.

I cocked my head to the side as if to ask what he meant but I already knew what he meant. I just wanted him to say it out loud.

"You just look a lot like Alana," Matt said, his eyes searching mine. His eyes seemed to get darker, sadness seeping into them. Peeling his gaze from mine, he started towards the living room. "Take a seat," he offered, his gaze distant.

Sitting in the nearest seat, I crossed my legs and smiled, almost flattered by his comment. "I really wish I knew what happened to her," I said, "Alana I mean. It's sad how she wasn't really given a second chance at anything." I looked up at him. "I'm sorry, I know you really loved her."

Matt nodded, a far off look in his blue eyes. Dragging his hand through his hair he nodded. "Yeah, I really did." He sat down beside me rather than across from me, immediately making me nervous.

"Did you love Angela too?" I asked suddenly, the question escaping my lips.

Matt narrowed his eyes, "what does it matter?" he asked.

"It's just weird," I blurted, "how one of your girlfriends goes missing and the other one dies a brutal death. They were both best friends." I shrugged, "And blonde and blue eyed." I didn't know why I said that. I didn't even know what I meant by that; it just slipped out.

"What are you getting at, Ivy?" Matt asked, his tone revealing his anger. He glared at me, his eyes darkening.

"I-I don't know," I stammered, dropping my gaze. "I'm not accusing you, I know you better than to know you wouldn't hurt them. It just makes me wonder exactly what happened there. Is it possible that Keith killed them? I know why he would have killed Alana. Did he have something against Angela too? Or maybe Angela killed Alana because of you..."

"What are you even doing here?" Matt snapped, "If you really just came here to accuse me or anyone close to me, you can leave. I'm not doing this right now."

"I'm sorry. I just don't know what to do," I said, "I'm obviously really shaken up and I'm sorry if I'm offending you, that's not my intention. I'm just trying to understand the situation. I really want to know what happened to my sister. And Angela."

Matt was silent for a second. He continued to glare at me, as if unsure of what to say. He seemed caught off guard. "Why would you think that I know?" He asked finally, turning to me.

"I'm just shaken up," I sighed, falling back into the couch. "And scared," I added. "I keep feeling like there should be answers.

Like there's something that I don't know and it's scaring me. I feel like I can be doing so much more."

"I wish I had the answers, Ivy, but I don't," Matt said. "I'm tired of people looking to me for answers. I don't know what happened, I wasn't part of it."

Nodding, I looked into Matt's innocent blue eyes. "I know."

Alana – Back to the party – (three months ago)

Matt had me pressed against Tanya's house, a look crossing his light eyes that I had never seen before and in an instant, my heart began to pound hard in my chest.

Brushing off my anxiety, I let out a burst of laughter, hoping to god it would ease his hands that were clenching at his sides. Confusion crossed Matt's face. "See, this is why we don't work anymore," I said, "your anger gets the best of you and I feel like I can't communicate with you when you're like this. This is why we went downhill." Wincing, I bit my tongue. It sounded better in my head. Out loud, it sounded like the poorly disguised lie that it was.

I knew him too well; nothing would work to calm him down now. There were too many reasons why I did what I did, but I couldn't tell him. What I saw or felt didn't matter to him anyway.

"Right. So since we can't communicate, you can justify fucking my best friend?" Matt asked, his eyes flaring.

Swallowing my laughter, my nerve endings began to tingle. I didn't know he knew that much.

181

He wasn't supposed to know that much. "How did you find out?" I murmured, avoiding eye contact.

Something changed in his features, "I didn't know for sure, I just assumed," Matt said, his face crushing with realization, "I guess now I know, don't I?" His eyes turned cold and dark with hatred. It was a look I had never seen before and in an instant, my heart began to race.

He shook his head. He turned around and ran his hand through his hair, what he always did when he was thinking. I could almost see the gears turning in his head.

It was time for me to leave. Every fiber of my body ached with a warning. He was going to blow up and I shouldn't be around for that. I took a step to the side. The sound of my footstep seemed to disturb the still, night air.

Registering the fact that I was leaving, Matt spun around at an inhuman pace. It was clear he didn't have a plan for what he was doing but his eyes darted around, looking for something. Finally, his eyes caught sight of a line of rope that was holding a tree up against a rod. The gears seemed to stop turning in his head. Every second slowed.

Suddenly, Matt gripped the rope and with a sudden rip he

got it loose before I could question his motives. There was something about the look in his eyes; something I had only caught glimpses of before, rage, unpredictability.

I turned around on wooden legs, my heart pounding in my throat. I ran towards the back door of Tanya's place but my arm was seized in seconds, as if Matt could read what I was thinking.

"I don't think so," Matt said, his tone sharp.

"No," I snapped, my voice shrill, "I can do what I want." My voice seemed like the defiant cry of a child; weak in comparison.

"Not right now you can't," Matt's grip on my wrist tightened into a painful twist. He forced my arm behind my back, holding me prisoner to whatever he would do next. Letting out a scream of shock, he pushed me forward with his free hand.

"Move," Matt demanded, his voice cold and emotionless.

"No!" I yelled. I opened my mouth to scream for help. Matt cut me short by pushing me forward into the grass. Pitching forward, I collapsed onto the manicured lawn. The sweet smell of the grass registered through my mind. I wished I were anywhere but there. My head spun with the impact.

Matt jumped on top of my back, craning my arm into an unnatural position. "Keep it up and I'll snap your arm in half, right

183

here," he whispered in my ear. A twinge of fear curdled in my stomach. His words made every bone in my body shake with dread.

"Understand?" Matt whispered, his hot breath seeming to burn my ear. I nodded, choking on the sweet smell of the fresh grass.

"Well just in case you don't..." Matt spun the thin rope around both of my wrists and pulled it taut.

"Matt, look at yourself! Are you really going to do this?" I cried, straining my wrists against the rope.

"Don't talk," Matt demanded. He jumped up and pulled me up with the jolt of his arm. He led me out the back gate, and shut it without making a sound.

We moved quietly through the woods before Matt's voice broke through the silence.

"Do you know what sucks about this?" he asked. I didn't answer. "I trusted you. You took me for who I was and we really loved each other. You made me feel normal and you made me feel like it was okay to be myself. And now I find this. It's hard to believe we loved each other. Because people who love each other don't treat one another like this, wouldn't you agree, Alana? So with that in mind, did you even really love me? Or was it all just a fucking game to you like everything else in your life?" His voice cracked. It was hard to even imagine him having emotion after this. The fact that he still did made me sick to my stomach.

"Of course I did," I whispered. That wasn't a lie. But it sounded meek and unsure.

"Liar," Matt snapped, pushing me roughly from behind. My foot caught a large tree root that was protruding out of the ground. Hitting the forest floor, all of the air escaped my lungs in one blow, leaving me temporarily winded and choking for air. My legs shook as I struggled to get them beneath me. I tried to get my upper torso up, my arms straining behind my back.

Craning my head around, I saw Matt, coming toward me, his expression hard. Letting out a scream of shock, I struggled into the soft dirt of the forest floor. The putrid smell of moss filled my nostrils; every sense was heightened.

"You really shouldn't be so clumsy," Matt said shaking his head in disgust. "Get up."

Struggling with my nerves, I did as he told me and bit my tongue, trying to hold back the snappy response that was boiling to the surface. "What are you doing?" I cried, the words slipping out of my mouth. "If you really loved me at all you wouldn't do this." My words sounded like a desperate plea. I couldn't help but be desperate.

His anger usually let up by now but it didn't.

Matt stopped and spun me around, pinning me to a tree. "I did love you, you know I did. That wasn't good enough for you, was it? Don't tell me I don't love you. You're the one who betrayed *me*!"

His response caught me off guard, so I stared at him, my mind blank. There was nothing I could say to make it better. There was nothing I could say to relax his features that were twisted up in an uncontrollable rage.

"I love you," I gasped. "I was just scared." Again it sounded frantic and weak. He would see right through it.

Shaking his head, Matt spat, "It's too late." Tears sprung to his eyes but vanished with a burst of anger that shot through him. He was conflicted but there was no way I could console him like this. His anger had taken over.

In one swift movement, Matt pulled me off the tree and pushed me forward. There was a hesitation in his grasp. He was getting weaker and it gave me hope. With that in mind, I continued forward, holding onto that hope with everything that I had.

"Alana, you ruined everything," Matt muttered, sounding defeated. He was leading me closer to my house and I felt my body tingle with anticipation.

If I had to fight I would. I just didn't want to because I felt like it was possible that I deserved what I had coming. I didn't know how hard I would fight, or how hard I could fight. Although my life was a mess of mistakes and horrible things that I had done, part of me was still holding onto what was right. I had hurt him. But it was too late to come to that realization, and far too inconvenient.

"We could have been together," Matt murmured, a sob choking his words. "I don't want to do this."

"Then don't," I said, turning around. "Please. We can work through this," I begged, tears stinging my eyes. "I really do love you."

Matt stared at me, stunned by my sudden outbreak of emotion. He appeared to be at a loss of words. Dread leaked into me as I saw his shock flip to anger. "STOP LYING TO ME!" Matt screamed, his face scarlet and dewy with sweat. He pushed me hard and I fell back but struggled to stay on my feet.

Spinning around, I threw myself forward, taking advantage of the second of freedom I had. Adrenaline coursed through my body as I leaped forward, winding around the trees and shrubs that loomed towards me like hands of my inevitable fate. Dodging them, I started to cry in desperation. I took a second to look behind me. I shouldn't have. Matt was tailing me quickly, which made every bit of hope leak out of me.

Still, I pushed forward, my lungs and throat aching with dry tension and searing pain.

Robeline - Trust

"You've always trusted Matt," Robeline said, writing it down as she spoke. "Why?"

Grimacing, I searched for answers. I never really knew why I trusted him. It was something that seemed so natural to me. "What does it matter?" I asked, kinking my head to the side and throwing her a sarcastic look. "How would that help you put anything together?"

Robeline stared at me, her face emotionless. She was waiting patiently for a response I wasn't too willing to give. Matt had nothing to do with what was going on. I knew that, she knew that. Why would she bring it up?

"Matt didn't do it," I muttered.

"How are you so sure?" Robeline asked, flipping her earlier question.

Smiling sarcastically, I pointed my left index finger at her. "I see what you did there," I laughed.

"Are you in love with

Matt?" Robeline probed, narrowing her small eyes.

"What? No!" I snapped.

"Don't you think if you were a little more honest with yourself about how you're feeling, it would release some tension and hatred you have for yourself?" Robeline asked, raising an eyebrow.

"Okay," I said finally, raising my hands in a truce. "It isn't what you think."

"There's no right or wrong answer, Ivy."

"Alana and Matt dated for a long time, okay? Of course I trusted him. I saw the way he acted with her. He really loved her. People don't hurt the ones they love."

"Love makes people do crazy things," Robeline stated. "What's the real reason?"

"That's still a very big part of why I trust him," I reasoned, irritated but relieved that she had seen through my half-truth. "When Alana used to…" I struggled with my words, "…put me down, Matt used to stand up for me."

"Stand up for you how?" Robeline asked.

Smiling, I thought back to the memories. "He just didn't take it. He wouldn't let Alana put me down in front of him. I think it was because he had been bullied at one time too and he knew how it hurt."

Robeline nodded, a half smile on her face. "Well that's very kind of him."

"It gave me a break from Alana and god knows I needed it," I laughed.

Robeline nodded, her eyes vacant for a second. I knew that meant she was about to ask me something that would make me uncomfortable.

"Now, did you by chance, follow Alana and Matt into the woods?" Robeline asked.

"No!" I snapped, "What kind of a question is that? I told you what happened."

"I'm just double checking," Robeline said, putting her pen down.

Ivy – Too soon

The air in the room seemed to still between Matt and I.

It was obvious that I trusted him, I wondered if he would pick up on it but it became apparent to me that he had considering the silence. It was probably too much. Part of me felt like it was time to let him know that he really helped me in my moments of need and that when he stood up for me, it really meant something to me. It made me trust him and stand by him because nobody was there for me and he was so willing. Even my family didn't pick me up after Alana had torn down my self-esteem.

Matt finally nodded, his blue eyes soft for a second, releasing all of my nerves at once. He turned to me, "I really appreciate that, Ivy, and it means a lot to me." His eyes lingered on mine, as if confused with my trust in him. The way he looked at me changed something inside me.

Butterflies whirled in my stomach and before I could understand what I was doing and why, my mouth was on his, kissing him, passionately. He kissed me back which eliminated all of my insecurity. I couldn't believe I was actually kissing him. Like I had wanted to for so long. I had held back because of circumstances and my insecurity and…Alana.

It was as if Matt had read my mind. He pulled away from me, his blue eyes angry. "Why did you do that?" he demanded and then stood up. He ran his fingers through his hair and looked out the window. He seemed to be rattled just as much as I was.

The reality of what I had done was beginning to sink in. Touching my lips, I winced in regret.

"Matt?" I asked, an apple growing in my throat. It was hard to tell whether I was upset because the kiss ended or that he didn't see me like 'that.' Like Alana. "I did not mean to do that, I guess I read the situation wrong and I just…" No excuse, "I'm sorry," I muttered, defeated. My urge was supposed to stay just that, regardless of whether Alana was around or not. God knows I would hear about it later from Alana's limbo anyway.

"I think you need to leave," Matt said, avoiding eye contact with me. He stood up in a hasty rage, his eyes darting towards the floor.

I opened my mouth to speak but found it difficult to find the right words to say. I wanted to ask why, why I wasn't good enough but Alana and Angela were. "Why?" I asked in a meek whisper after, struggling with the question myself.

"Keep in mind, you were the one who reamed me out about dating Angela after Alana's disappearance and here you are doing the exact same thing. What sense does that make?" Matt demanded.

I opened my mouth to speak but found that I was at a loss of words. I didn't understand my actions and there was really no explanation. A few months ago, I would have never acted on an urge let alone one that would destroy my sister. But it felt like the urge was too strong and Alana couldn't do anything about it because she was gone. I just wanted to have that part in my life, that part where I was the girl who got kissed. I was acting selfish.

It was expected because I couldn't hold up a front anymore. I was always so careful to be considerate while growing up. I couldn't take it anymore. Now it was backfiring on me.

Embarrassed, I stood up carefully because I was light headed and started to the door. It felt like every second after that was one of the most awkward moments of my life. I felt like a dog that had just gotten scolded and now I was leaving with my tail between my legs. I thought I was over feeling that way. I thought I had grown and changed and I was different... better. Was I better or was that just the illusion I gave myself?

I would never know why I was rejected but it could be anything. Maybe it was just Alana and the fact that I was her sister and I acted poorly or maybe it was something a little harder to admit like maybe I just wasn't good enough no matter what I did.

I started to step outside, not even bothering to say goodbye when Matt grabbed my wrist and I spun around in shock.

Matt must have seen the pain in my eyes because his eyes softened. "It's too soon," he murmured, and then smiled half-heartedly as if expecting me to believe him. But then again, I did, maybe because I melted in his halfhearted apology or maybe because he was the only one I trusted out of Alana's friends.

Ivy – Rejection

It was becoming a sickness of mine, trying to reveal what had happened and why. Nothing was coming together and making sense. So, on a journey to illuminate the situation in our town, I started towards Tanya's house. I hadn't been there since the night of her party when my sister had vanished out of the blue and part of me was scared to go back, to remember that night and to reveal something I maybe had forgotten before. There was something about what had happened that wasn't adding up.

Taking a deep breath, I knocked on her door. It felt so strange. It wasn't like I was a friend of hers. In fact, I really despised her on account of my sister. But Tanya had a real reason to hate my sister, which made her an obvious suspect in my mind. And here I was, facing the situation head on.

Tanya swung the door open and then scowled the second her eyes fell on me. She looked me over through the screen door, her eyes surveying me in blatant disgust. I knew what she was thinking. I looked like Alana and it was pathetic of me to try so hard. I could see the wheels turning in her head.

Annoyed by her reaction, I cocked my head to the side and smiled. "Mind if I come in?"

Tanya tucked her upper lip up in a fake smile. "I guess," she muttered, pressing the screen door open and then letting it drop before I could grab it. She spun around and strolled into her house.

"Thanks," I muttered, catching the door and forcing it open.

"What do you want?" Tanya asked, picking up glasses and plates that were scattering her place. It was apparent to me that Keith had moved in with her and he was leaving the place a huge mess. A half-eaten piece of pizza lingered on the glass coffee table and I stared at it in silence. My confidence was starting to dwindle.

"I just wanted to talk," I said.

Tanya stopped abrupt in her tracks and looked up at me, a look of disgust crossing her face. "Since when do we *talk*?"

Flustered, I snapped my gaze away from her glare. "Well, I don't know-"

"What's the real reason you're here, Ivy?" Tanya asked, shifting her weight. She tossed the dishes into the sink and looked up at me impatiently for an answer. "You're wasting my time," she

197

snapped. "And what the fuck did you do to your hair? I mean it looks better than it was, but fuck, that's really not saying much."

Wincing, I absorbed her comment and then shoved it into the back of my mind, not willing to deal with more blows to my confidence. Thinking back to the real reason I was there, I dove right in, "There's a lot of things that aren't adding up with these… murders," I admitted, pealing my gaze from Tanya's dark glare.

"What's your point?" Tanya asked, her voice reaching an octave louder. Silence set into the room. Her dark eyes seemed to cut into me.

"Oh, of course, you think *I* know," Tanya said finally, letting out a bark-like laugh. "Typical behavior of your sister, I just didn't know you two were so much alike."

"I just want to know what happened," I muttered.

"So now you care, hey?" Tanya's smile grew as she watched my reaction.

I stepped forward, "I think you know something." It was a wonder why I hadn't suspected her before. If anything, Tanya was Alana's worst enemy. Grinding my teeth, I braced myself for Tanya's anger.

"Fuck off," Tanya muttered, rolling her eyes and spinning

around, the plate with the slice of half eaten pizza in hand.

Taking a deep breath, I tried to hold the pent up frustration that started to explode from my chest. "I just want to talk."

"No you don't, Ivy, you want someone to blame for your precious sister's disappearance. You want to make yourself feel better by meddling." Tanya shook her head, "What the hell is wrong with you?"

"Excuse me?" I demanded, stepping closer to her. "I have no idea who killed my sister and my friend and I just want answers, but you have to turn it around like it's wrong for wanting some closure."

Tanya laughed, "Do you actually think Angela considered you a friend?" she asked, her eyebrows flickering up with amusement.

Blinking with shock, my fists balled at my side.

"Oh you do," Tanya laughed, "Aw that's sweet, I bet she would be flattered."

With a burst of anger that seemed to unleash itself at that moment, I found myself across the room, inches from Tanya, ready to throw her on the ground. Just as I was about to pull my fist back and throw it into Tanya's face, I was interrupted.

"What in the hell is going on here?" Keith demanded,

standing at the entrance of the kitchen. He was in green pajama pants, shirtless. Typical. His eyes danced with laughter and a smile began to twitch at the sides of his mouth. "Were you guys really going to fight?" he asked before anyone could respond.

"This psycho came here to accuse me of killing Angela and Alana," Tanya spat, her dark eyes flaring at the sight of me.

It occurred to me then that it probably wasn't a good idea to fight Tanya. She looked like she could throw me down and beat the life out of me from just a look. Of course that thought came afterwards. Even though moments earlier, I threw myself at her, ready to pound the smug smile off of her face.

Keith looked me over, "Nice hair," he smiled, his eyes crinkling at the sides. "Looks hot."

Tanya shot a look of shock and irritation at Keith that wiped the smile off of his face. Considering the circumstances that he and Tanya had dealt with earlier, comments like that really worked against him. Especially because I was the sister of the girl that had drove a wedge in their relationship.

Seeming to sense the tension in the room, Keith changed the topic. "What brings you here?" he asked, lighthearted, but slightly annoyed.

Tanya scowled at him. "I told you, Keith, she's accusing me of killing her sister. Don't you ever listen?" she snapped then her eyes fell on me, full of pure hatred. "Don't tell me you're screwing around with this skank now."

Incredulous, Keith and I exchanged a glance of shock and then looked at Tanya.

"Tanya, I'm not trying to get in between anyone here," I said, narrowing my eyes at her.

"That's exactly something *she* would say," Tanya spat. I didn't have to question who she was talking about.

"I'm not Alana," I said.

"No, at least Alana was straight up. You're worse," Tanya shot back, cutting at my self-esteem.

"Take it easy," Keith said, placing a hand on Tanya's shoulder. She shrugged it off, her dark eyes still burning into me. She flipped her long thick hair over her shoulder, not breaking eye contact with me.

"Did you really come here to talk about Alana?" Keith asked, his expression revealing his irritation. It was obvious he didn't want to talk about Alana, especially with Tanya there to harass him about it. I wondered why they didn't break up over it.

"I'm just searching for answers," I said finally. "Not a lot of what I know adds up. I just wish…" I paused, trying to gather my thoughts. "I wish I had some closure."

Keith shook his head. "Well you're not going to find it here," he said. His green eyes burned into mine. "Why don't you just drop it?"

"I can't."

"Well don't come here 'searching for answers,' Ivy. We don't want to talk about it. Just drop it and leave it well enough alone for god's sake. You're stirring up the pot with Tanya and I both."

I took a deep breath in attempt to control the bubble of anger that was growing inside me, threatening to blow up. "Both of you should have been suspects," I shouted, my face growing hot. The look that they gave me… I couldn't stop. "You killed Alana because she had your boyfriend. Or maybe the two of you did this together."

"You little bitch, you have some nerve," Tanya snapped, rage erupting from her and she pounced on me before I could even blink.

Falling to the floor, I clawed at Tanya's face and then pushed at her shoulders. She yanked at my hair. It was the 'typical' girl fight but I had never been in a fight before and I really didn't know what to do. She eased up on me easier than I thought. Then I realized Keith had picked her up by the waist and pulled her behind him.

"Whoa," Keith said, holding his hands out in front of me. "Enough with the fighting," he demanded, looking behind him and Tanya.

Standing up in a huff, I straightened my clothes and brushed my hair behind my shoulder. "Tanya just can't handle the fact that I'm catching onto her, or you two, whoever the hell killed my sister," I said, my voice shaking. "Tanya knew about you and my sister," I said, staring at Keith and enjoying the uneasy look that crossed his face.

"She knew about it the night that my sister went missing."

Keith opened his mouth to speak but didn't. "We dealt with it and it's really not any of your business."

"My sister is my business," I shot back at Keith, glaring at him. "And I have every right to suspect both of you. The way you two are reacting just confirms my suspicion."

"Seriously!" Tanya started up from behind Keith. "Suddenly you're a wanna-be cop?"

Keith held up his hand at her. "Let's all relax and stop

throwing accusations around," he said, staring hard at me. "I don't know what your problem is Ivy but we've had enough, please leave,"

Rolling my eyes, I turned around and started for the door. "Thanks for your time," I muttered, glaring at Tanya. My eyes lingered on Keith who stared at me wide eyed. I turned and left.

~

Exhausted, I collapsed on the couch. I was home alone, again. It was something I was becoming accustomed to. It didn't even bother me anymore.

My eyes fell to a photo of my parents together. They were both smiling. Funny how I didn't really remember them. It always bothered me that I didn't remember anything. I stared at my mother's face. She had the same smile as Alana. It was too bad I didn't get any of my looks from my mother.

I couldn't pull my eyes away. Transfixed, I stared at her bright red lips.

I thought back to a memory I had of my parents before the car crash. The only memory I had was being in the back seat of my parent's car, driving me to dance class. There was something new in the memory. When my mother turned around to look at me, there was something different, something that any oblivious child would brush off. My mother's smile was fake, like forcing a grimace as if she were angry that she had to come along to gymnastics that day. It looked like she just might throw a tantrum like Alana was known to do. God, they were so much alike.

But her smile. It was all that I could focus on. Her red lips bending awkwardly, finalizing my doubt towards her. It was always there.

Suddenly, I was thrown into a vivid flashback.

My parents were in their bedroom, arguing. They probably figured we wouldn't hear them by the cartoons blaring in the background. Alana and I were smarter then they set us up to be. Alana enjoyed oblivion. She was sitting into front of the TV on the worn out floral couch. I didn't know why, but I was in front of the door, listening. Most of it was jumbled together in an angry mess of commotion.

"WHY!" I heard my mother yell. "Why would I forgive you, when we have a daughter that is constantly reminding me of what you did *wrong*?"

There was silence. I registered the words for a second. I didn't understand back then but seeing it again, I understood. I couldn't breathe.

"She's a child, she doesn't deserve that," my father said. He was defending *me*.

"Every time I look at her, I'm reminded of what you did wrong. She's a reminder of why I shouldn't be with you. God, I don't know why I'm still with you. Everyone knows she isn't mine. They don't see me in her."

"Why would you stay with me if you couldn't get over this? You knew what this would entail when we decided to stay together. If you couldn't take it, you shouldn't have been wasting my time telling me that you could!" My father's voice boomed, as he started to shuffle objects around in the room.

"Well, I'm not fit to be the parent of two kids. Or maybe I just lack the maternal instincts to look after a daughter that isn't mine," my mother whined, breaking into soft crying moments afterwards.

"I'm sorry," my father said. "This is my responsibility now. I'm sorry that this fell on you, Sharon, but she doesn't know any other mother than you. You can't reject her, it's not fair to her. Please, we can work on this. I'm not the same man I was when I was 25, you have to know that."

The deafening silence grew in the room, breaking only by

the soft cries of my mother. The door opened and she stepped out, her blond hair disheveled. Her eyes fell on me and she jumped in shock and wiped the tears from her eyes hurriedly. "Oh, honey!"

That was all she could say.

How could I have repressed that?

Alana - Morals

There are certain unspoken morals that people generally have. Take for example, trying to get with your dead sisters' ex. That might be crossing the line, if you have any morals that is. In most cases, this would be labeled as "common sense." Turns out, it's not as common.

Sitting on Ivy's bed, I looked around the room, taking in her everyday items. I spotted my perfume bottle sitting on her dresser. Anger pounded through my body as I strolled up to it. It was true that I was dead and she may as well use my stuff but part of me wanted to throw Ivy across the room. She wasn't the same and she was trying to be like *me*. She wanted my boyfriend, my clothes, my look, my friends, even my hair color. It had gone too far.

Opening Ivy's drawers, I sifted through the clothes. Mine, mine, mine, and of course, *mine*. It was as if she threw out all of her old clothes and replaced them with mine. I slammed the drawer shut.

Ivy walked into her room and her brown eyes fell upon me. She dropped her bag and avoided eye contact. She looked guilty. Exhausted and empty, but mostly guilty. There was something different in her eyes. She looked ready to defend herself. This would start a fight. She was hiding something that I already knew because I was *there*.

"So," I grabbed the perfume bottle and raised it up in the air and then crashed it down on the dresser with a thud. "You're really trying to take over my life aren't you?" I demanded.

Ivy shook her head, her blonde hair falling out of her ponytail. "It's not like that, you know it isn't," she muttered, straightening the perfume bottle. She sighed and looked up at herself if the mirror.

"No," I snapped, shaking my head. "I saw you with Matt." I collapsed onto the bed.

Ivy's face grew pale in the mirror, she dropped her gaze. "You don't understand," she rambled, her cheeks started to turn red. "I-I was always in your shadow and I wasn't ever allowed to experiment with makeup or clothes or even guys because you would get mad at me."

"So that makes this okay?" I asked, cocking my head to the side. "Do you have any idea how stupid that sounds?"

"It doesn't make it okay," Ivy said, looking down at her hands. "I know that. I was selfish and I seemed to forget about everything in that moment, I just wanted to experiment."

"On my boyfriend?" I yelled. Taking a deep breath, I shook my head. "This isn't normal. None of this is *normal*."

"You didn't want him anyway," Ivy snapped, her face flushing.

"Listen carefully," I snapped through gritted teeth, "You kissed *my* boyfriend."

"And you're dead," she shrugged and looked down. She shook her head, "I-I didn't mean that," she murmured, her face falling into her hands. She rubbed her face, leaving it pink. "I'm too tired to deal with this right now."

"Yeah," I muttered, standing up, "maybe this is why you can't sleep, because you can't live with what you've turned into." Ivy's face didn't change. She continued to stare at me with a look of exhaustion, as if to ask how long I would drag this out. Irritated, I continued. "This is why I hated you growing up. Underneath that front that you try so hard to keep up, I knew that you were a selfish, conceited little bitch. *You* killed mom and dad," I murmured, savoring the look that came over Ivy's face. That was the look I wanted.

The door was thrown open before Ivy could defend herself.

Gran burst in. Crossing my legs, I leaned back onto the bed, confident with the fact that she couldn't see me.

"Ivy, who are you talking to?" Gran asked, her soft eyes expressing her shock and concern. "W-were you just arguing with yourself?"

Ivy shook her head, still hurt by my words. Finally, she spun away from the mirror and faced Gran "I-uh," she paused her face falling, "Why are you so concerned?" She asked finally. "You haven't been concerned about me since the day Alana went missing. What does it matter to you now?"

Gran stood in shocked silence.

"Really," Ivy muttered, tears beginning to fall down her face.

Gran opened her mouth to speak but seemed at a loss for words.

Ivy wiped her face with her sleeve and then grabbed her bag and ran for the door.

Robeline – Losing yourself

"I guess that must've hurt," Robeline concluded, her eyes trained on her notes.

Blinking at the tears that were forming in my eyes, I avoided her stare. "What do you think?" I said, swallowing the apple of emotion that flooded up my throat. If I let it flow too high it would choke me out. I had already spilled too much. Raising my index finger to my mouth, I chewed at the nail, hoping the motion would subside my nerves.

"Would you agree that you had lost yourself?" Robeline asked, narrowing her eyes and cocking her head, a hint of sympathy touching her eyes.

"There wasn't anything that made me myself to begin with," I said, folding my hands in my lap. It was hurting too much to chew my nails. My index finger started to bleed. I continued with my explanation, "Like I told you, I was lost in life. I wasn't anything special. I had been bullied my whole life. So I guess I transformed into something I never really

thought I would be or have the power to be. It felt good for a while –
to actually be someone. I lost control... Eventually. Maybe I was
stupid to think that I wouldn't. Even Alana lost control of her life."

My mind wandered back to those nights where I pretended
everything was alright by diving into other subjects to keep my mind
busy. I avoided the fact that I didn't know who I was or what I stood
for or why I didn't have any friends. It was easier to avoid it because
it didn't make sense to let it destroy me. But when I started to turn
into a different person and identify myself with makeup and clothes
and my sister's friends, I lavished in the 'new me', because anything
was better than the old me. For my whole life, I was told I wasn't
good enough, not pretty enough, not smart enough, not liked enough.
How, exactly could I be comfortable with myself let alone *like*
myself?

Robeline sat in uncomfortable silence as I tried to pull my
emotions back together. It was embarrassing that I was losing control
of that too. It was something I thought I was able to control because I
had no one to talk to. I had bottled my thoughts and feelings up.

"Now with your grandparents," Robeline paused, "they
seemed to be stuck in their own little world after your sister went
missing which only lead you to feel more alone. Is this an issue you

213

didn't feel was important enough to bring up to them?"

I shook my head, "No, not really. My sister was dead. How were my emotions even applicable? They were grieving. I couldn't just beg for attention." How real was that to admit!

"You're worthy of that you know," Robeline murmured, "You're important too."

I shook my head and averted my eyes.

Robeline looked up at me. "Are we okay to continue?"

Nodding, I forced my hands up to my eyes and wiped away the tears that had poured out of my eyes and down my face with a rush of emotion.

Robeline seemed to sense that it was time to change the subject. "Do you remember anything else about how your parents treated you?" Robeline asked.

"I don't remember my parents, I told you that," I stated, intertwining my fingers together.

"Why don't you remember?" Robeline asked as she scribbled something down.

Shrugging, I unlaced my fingers. "I'm forgetful, flaky, stupid. Who knows?"

Robeline started to write down what I had said. "The one

thing you do remember is that you weren't biologically your mother's daughter. How did you take that?"

"Fine."

Robeline nodded, as if understanding that she wasn't going to get anywhere with that. "I suppose that's a touchy subject but I'd expect nothing less."

She flipped back a few pages and looked up at me. "I hate to call you out on this, Ivy, but you lied to me about your feelings for Matt."

"So what?" I shook my head, "What was I supposed to say? I was in love with my sister's boyfriend? How does that not look bad from where I stand?"

"Ivy, I need the truth," Robeline said, "Not something that sounds better. You can't hide behind lies or you will drown in them."

"It was just easier," I muttered, fiddling with my fingers.

"Of course it's easier," Robeline murmured, "It's human nature to protect yourself but some things have to be said. If I outright ask you a question, from now on, I want a straight up answer."

A flood of heat and anger washed through me.

"There's no reason to lie. This is a safe place," Robeline

continued. She looked down at her notes, reviewing my story. "Now why did you blame Tanya and Keith for killing Alana?" She asked, raising her eyebrows.

"Why wouldn't I?" I laughed, crossing my arms. "They're obvious suspects. My sister was screwing Keith and Tanya knew about it. And what Tanya said at the party at the beginning rings a few warning bells."

"Were you stretching the truth at all?" Robeline asked.

"Of course not!" I raged. "Why don't you believe me?" I shook my head. "That's not the only reason I don't trust her. It's obvious Tanya is an overly jealous girlfriend, who knows what she is actually capable of. How aren't you suspicious of her?"

"On a bias level, I suppose I can understand your suspicion," Robeline murmured, writing down something.

"Or maybe Keith was avenging his girlfriend, after all, he did feel guilty about him and Alana," I concluded.

Robeline nodded and continued to scribble on her notepad.

"Now one more question," Robeline stated, her pen stopping abruptly on her notepad. "Did you follow Alana and Matt into the woods the night of the party?" She asked.

"You already asked that," I muttered.

"I feel like I wasn't getting the full truth," Robeline explained, "Just nod yes or no."

I was uncomfortable with the question but she already knew. Nodding my head, I looked away from her scrutinizing gaze to her notepad. I couldn't make it out.

Robeline didn't mutter a word about it, she wrote it down and then changed the subject. "Are you ready to continue?" she asked, raising her eyebrows and placing her pen on the notebook.

Falling back into the chair, I hid my embarrassment for being snoopy. "Of course."

Ivy - Confrontation

I could see myself making coffee. It was like a cartoon. There was a disconnect between my mind and my body. I was drifting slightly above myself, watching, as if it were normal to experience that type of hallucination.

It was clear that lack of sleep was affecting my ability to get through the day. The image of myself scooped out two heaping tablespoons of dark roast and dumped it into the filter. Grinds of coffee escaped the spoon as I jolted, shaken from the nerve-struck state I was in. I was back in my body.

Taking in a deep breath, I shook my head and looked down at my hands that were trembling. Maybe caffeine wasn't the best self-remedy considering I had already had a few cups. Caffeine had become my medicine.

Staring at the mountains on the cup, I struggled to control the impending panic attack. I was on the edge, threatening a relapse. My heart raced in my chest, counteracting my struggle to slow my breathing.

I ran the coffee pot under the tap. The water was brown, but I didn't seem to have the energy to care. I dumped it into the coffee maker and slammed the pot back in, pressing start.

"Looks like someone is on edge today," Grandpa's voice said.

My heart jumped into my throat for a second as I turned around to find him walking into the room, an empty glass in hand.

Grandpa laughed. "Maybe you've had too much coffee," he said, opening the dishwasher and placing the glass on the top rack.

"How else am I supposed to stay awake?" I said, pulling my hand over my face.

"Well it's late afternoon," Grandpa said, "Caffeine isn't going to help with sleep. Maybe you should be focusing on tackling that issue you seemed to have developed."

Nodding absently, I turned around to pour the hot coffee into my mug. "Can I ask you something?" I asked, my face turning red at the question that was seeming to pound at my skull, begging to be let out.

Grandpa was quiet for a moment. "Of course you can."

"I'm not mom's daughter, am I?" I asked, raising my eyes to the cupboard, focusing on the grooves on the wood and bracing for an answer I didn't know whether I was ready to hear.

"Ivy, you are your mother's daughter," Grandpa said slowly, deliberately. As if that could change reality.

I spun around and propped my elbows on the counter. "No, I'm not. I know I'm not. That's why I was treated differently my whole life. Even by my parents."

Grandpa sighed and sat down at the table.

I moved to the edge of the table, too nervous to sit down. "Why would you say that I looked like Sharon if she wasn't even my mother?" I asked.

Grandpa shook his head. "There are similarities in you that remind me of Sharon. In saying that, there doesn't have to be a blood relation. All I meant by that was you looked like you had something to say. Sharon was often tortured by her thoughts too."

"I don't understand why you would say that, knowing that I would find out that we weren't even blood-related," I said, pressing the palm of my hand into my temple.

"Because there's more to a child than blood, people who raise a kid have more of an impact between morals, between thoughts and between ideas. Sharon was lost in her mind a lot of the time and it made us feel like we had failed her as parents. She didn't have the confidence to speak her mind. I was scared we had sent you down the same road."

"Don't blame yourselves," I snapped, immediately irritated at my own response. Part of me wanted to say that it was their fault, to have something to pin my problems on. The reality of that was that I didn't know who to blame my problems on. But seeing grandpa withered in blame towards himself made me come to his defense.

Grandpa seemed to sense the hostility in my voice and continued, "There are many reasons why we didn't want you to know."

"Like what?" I asked, shaking my head. "If I would have known, at least I would have had somewhat of an understanding. Everything seems to add up now. Why I was treated differently from Alana and why we looked so different..."

"It isn't something we wanted you to be bothered by. It is far in the past and it shouldn't affect you now, it wasn't supposed to, you were supposed to be treated the same as your sister but I guess Sharon had a hard time accepting the fact that your father had a child outside of the marriage. It was hard on her. She leaned a lot on your grandmother during the process. While your parents were dealing with the infidelity and fixing their marriage, they found out about you."

"Who was my birth mother?" I asked, pulling out a chair and falling into it.

"She was young," Grandpa said, folding his hands on the table.

Frozen in shock, I leaned forward. "Who was she? How did my father meet her?"

Grandpa looked down at the table. "Your father went back to school to be an electrician. He met your birth mother there, they started out as friends and I suppose one thing lead to another. Of course, your father was already married to Sharon and had Alana at that time. Anyway, Sharon found out about it and stopped him from seeing her. Your birth mother-"

"What's her name?" I asked.

"It doesn't matter, she wasn't ready to have you," Grandpa said, his voice gruff and louder than he probably intended.

"What's her name?" I demanded.

Grandpa unfolded his hands, hesitant. "Her name is Katherine. She was going to place you up for adoption but your father wouldn't let it happen. He couldn't imagine a better place for you to be then with him and Sharon. I don't think you need me to tell you that that complicated things between your parents."

Shaking my head, I leaned forward. "Why would he do that?" I asked, in sudden disgust with my father.

"People make mistakes," Grandpa said, "I want you to know that you were always loved. Regardless of blood, you will always be *our* granddaughter."

"Sometimes it doesn't feel like it," I said.

Grandpa nodded and took my hand. "I know, and I'm sorry. The news of your sister really shook your grandmother up. She's a good woman with good intentions; you know that. She doesn't know how to act right now. I don't think either of us do."

It wasn't even the time frame. I was always treated differently and I sensed it. But it was too much to say. Too awkward and forthcoming. So I pressed my lips together.

"You will *always* be our granddaughter."

Touched by my grandpa's words, a smile grew over my face.

Suddenly, the screen door creaked open. That was my cue to leave. Craning around in my chair, I saw Gran struggling with opening the door, paper grocery bags in her arms. Grandpa got up to help.

I stood up in haste, swooping my coffee up with me. Not

today. She wasn't going to ruin a good thing today.

Escaping through the balcony door, I emerged into the cool autumn air. Drinking in the fresh air, I plopped down on the balcony chair. Sipping my coffee, I cringed at the sweetness; it was nauseating. It was, however, my fifth or sixth cup. Setting my cup back down, I thought through the conversation that was still fresh in my mind. Something about the chilling air seemed to wake me up.

My thoughts wavered back to Alana. It was obvious that I had done enough to piss her off. But then again, welcome to my life. Disappointment was something I had experienced over and over. Maybe she deserved to feel it. Of course, losing her life would have been a bigger disappointment than I have ever experienced. She still deserved it.

That was something I didn't want to say about the fight. That one time where I betrayed her and crossed a major line for her – she had done that to me too many times to count, wounding my self-esteem and leaving me to feel like I was worth nothing.

Any time I told Alana about a crush I had on someone in school, she was the first to approach the boy and flirt with them non-stop. She got the guy. Every time. It was hard to pretend like that didn't create the monster of what she was. And although I was done with thinking about that, it was the action that hurt. That she spited me that much to go ahead and do something that would hurt me. Not even for the fact that she happened to like that person too, but the fact that she did it to hurt me, to knock me down a peg. To show me I wasn't worthy of anything more. Of course, that was something she would never understand. And I would never say. So what did it matter?

My mind wandered as I sat outside on the deck. Hot cup of coffee in hand, I stared out into the woods and remembered everything that I had gone through with Alana. She was everything I despised, yet, I couldn't seem to stop wishing that I was like her.

The door creaked open behind me as I swallowed a gulp of coffee, noting how it felt as it seared down my throat. It didn't even hurt. Not willing to even say hello, I continued to look out into the woods.

Gran stepped in front of me. "Hi,"

Continuing to look ahead, I avoided looking at her, not in the mood for whatever she had to say. It was a childish thing to do but I couldn't seem to help myself. I didn't want to talk, and especially not to her.

After another second of silence that felt like a full minute,

Gran started to speak. "I know I have been… neglecting you," Gran struggled with the word. "I've been going though a lot with all that has happened. I've been mourning so much I guess I forgot to remind myself that you're going through the same thing," Gran forced a smile as tears formed along her lower lash line.

I didn't react.

Gran grabbed my hands from across the table. "I am so sorry Ivy, I really wish you had told me sooner that you were feeling this way, it was unfair of me to neglect you." Gran took a deep breath and then started heaving and fighting her tears. She took her hands from mine to wipe her tears.

Taking a deep breath, I peeled my gaze from her weeping figure. "It's alright," I said, praying for the crying to stop. I could probably mock that exact cry if I tried.

Gran tried to gather her emotions in a hurry, seeing that I wasn't sympathizing with her. She sniffled and silence overcame us. I was grateful for the silence but every time there was a sound, it seemed to shatter it and make me acutely aware of how uncomfortable I was with Gran sitting across from me crying. And I had nothing to say.

"Maybe it isn't such a bad idea to seek therapy?" Gran said

suddenly, breaking the silence. "It might be good for you to help you sort out the things that you are going through. You can talk to them about Alana and what you're going through," Gran paused, waiting for my reaction.

I didn't have a reaction.

"I know you haven't been sleeping well since Alana's been missing," Gran informed me, as if she was proud to have gathered the information in her zombie-like slumber. "Just think about it," she said, standing up.

"I will," I said, transfixed on my cup.

Gran leaned over and peered into my mug, "What is that, coffee?" she asked, shocked.

I nodded.

"I thought that was more Alana's typical drink," Gran murmured.

"Well you'd know that I drink coffee if you paid more attention," I muttered, taking a sip from the cup.

Gran stood in stunned silence. At a loss for words, she turned and left.

Robeline – Digging for answers

"And so you ended up here," Robeline murmured, setting her pen down and lifting her coffee to her lips. It would be cold by now. I cringed as she took a sip, as if too lost in thought to notice or care. Her eyes seemed glassy as she stared at me, waiting. Waiting for a reaction or for me to say or do anything.

"Here I am," I said, looking around the small room. My eyes fell to the cracked paint near the bottom of the wall.

"Funny how there was no conflict," Robeline murmured. "There was no ah-ha moment for you, no realization."

"What do you mean?" I asked.

"There are quite a few things that are not quite connecting with your story," Robeline stated, her glassy eyes looking intensely into mine. "That's what I mean."

"I'm telling the truth," I stated, crossing my arms stiffly across my chest.

"Oh I have absolutely no doubt in my mind that you are," Robeline murmured. "And   that's actually the scary part."

228

Averting my gaze, I started to snap the sole of my shoe against the floor. The repetition seemed to bring me back to reality. It was soothing in a weird way, like the clock was. It seemed like everything was spinning out of control and anything with something of a steady beat was all I could focus on.

Robeline didn't move for a few moments. She reviewed the notebook in front of her, "Do you mind if I ask you a couple questions about where we are so far?"

"I don't understand why you would need to review, I told you everything in the most explicit detail. There is nothing I left out," I growled a whine creeping into my voice. I didn't like that.

"Starting from the beginning now, when you first ran into your sister in her room, it scared you. Why?" Robeline asked, tilting her head. Her eyes bore into mine, revealing her confusion.

"Why?" I spat, "Why do you think? My dead sister shows up after three months, wouldn't anyone be scared?"

"But see, that's the thing," Robeline said, shaking her head as she reviewed her notes again, her eyes scanning the paper at a ridiculous speed. "Nobody knew she was dead. She was only missing. But you described yourself as being scared when you saw her."

My face seemed to twitch with the realization of what she was saying. Rubbing my hand over my face, I took a deep breath. "There was speculation that Alana was dead," I said, taking a deep breath, "And I told you it was a relief when she was gone," I murmured, avoiding eye contact.

"Speculation isn't good enough. Explain to me how you felt so much of relief in her absence that when she arrived back at home you fell back into the hallway and whispered 'no,' repeatedly to calm yourself? Seems like a bit of an overreaction, wouldn't you agree?" Robeline's eyes probed into mine, searching for answers. It made me uncomfortable.

"I hadn't seen her in so long, I guess I was shocked," I said reasoning with why I reacted that way. My stomach tilted with the firm look that Robeline gave me.

"Can I ask you a question?" Robeline asked.

"No, but I'm sure you're going to ask anyway," I muttered, pealing my gaze from her eyes.

"What happened before you got here?"

Ivy – The facility

It wasn't like I was the type to have secrets, after all, what would I hide? It wasn't like I was overly anxious about people snooping through my stuff but there was something in me that snapped when I saw Gran in my room, rummaging through my stuff. She was bent over by my nightstand by my bed when I walked in.

"What do you think you're doing?" I asked, my voice cutting through the quiet air.

Gran stood up straight, her eyes wide.

"What are you doing?!" I demanded, louder this time. Gran seemed to twitch at my anger.

"I was gathering laundry…" Gran started.

"That's not where my laundry is," I said, my jaw stiff. It was obvious Gran was nervous about something. Looking over my shoulder, I peered over at my laundry basket by the door. The clothes had been taken out and put into the laundry basket that Gran was using. She was half telling the truth, but that wasn't good enough.

Then my eyes fell upon

the jeans that I had worn *that night*, the night I had snuck out to go to the party that Alana was going to. Those jeans had been sitting in the bottom of my laundry hamper for months; the shirt and hoodie was paired with them. I didn't get to washing them; I had left it. I really didn't know why.

Gran shook her head, her blue eyes watery. "Ivy, what's going on?"

"Nothing. I don't know what you're talking about." I felt backed into a wall. It was why I demanded privacy. Of course, Gran was the type to break down those barriers. I should have known this would happen.

"There's blood all over those clothes over there," Gran said, her hand flying up to her mouth. She held it as if she was scared to cry. "What happened?"

"How do you know its blood? It's probably a stain, maybe I cut myself."

Gran nodded, tears in her eyes. "You cut yourself," she said.

Shrugging, I held back my anger, "What do you think I did?" I demanded.

Gran didn't look at me; she stared at the floor in silence.

"You think I killed someone," I stated in blank realization.

"You know what I think?" I demanded, storming towards my clothes in the hamper. Throwing them one by one into my closet I felt rage forcing it's way through me. Tears sprang to my eyes. "I think you're looking for a reason to lock me away, in fact, I know you are. 'I just want you to have someone to talk to,' are you kidding me? You could have been that person, Gran, but you chose not to. You chose to wallow in grief," I spat, tears spewing from my eyes.

"My daughter and granddaughter died," Gran cried, her voice shaking at a high octave.

"And you neglected the rest of your family. Did you forget I was also your granddaughter, or does it bother you that I'm not blood like Alana?"

Gran didn't reply.

"My god, is this really about me not being related to you by blood?"

Gran shook her head, tears welling in her eyes. "Explain to me why you have this," she said, shaking her head as if in disbelief. She lifted up a long silver knife with an encrusted handle from behind her.

"I've never seen that before," I shook my head, "It's not mine," I yelled, making deliberate eye contact that wavered because of her penetrating stare. I kept my arms crossed in front of me, trying to control the shakes that were beginning in my legs. In a rage, I turned around, and ran out of the house.

~

There was nothing to say on the car ride there. I had no reasoning, nothing that would make anyone believe me. Alana had set me up, that was apparent. It wasn't like I had the option to talk about that without making it seem like I should be locked away. I'd already proved that point. Or Alana had.

Instead, I peered out the back window at the streets of my hometown. I admired the beauty of the trees and the scenery. Even I knew that this was the last time I would see my hometown for a while. Grandpa was driving, his expression solemn in the rear view mirror. Gran hadn't said a word since finding the knife. The car was too silent. Grandpa hadn't even turned on the radio. He was still in shock.

It was apparent to me that that was Alana's way to get back at me. She was malicious and deceiving like that. Her payback was always awful. I knew that after this many years.

The drive seemed endless. Although I knew where I was going, part of me didn't want to believe it. It was better to live in blind oblivion, with the way that life worked out for me. It was better not to think. With this in mind, I plugged in my ear buds and leaned back, letting dreams of hell envelope me.

~

Opening my eyes, I looked around at my surroundings. Nearly pressing my face on the glass, I looked up at what looked like an institution. My mind still numb with sleep, I managed to unbuckle myself but I was still in no shape to get out of the vehicle. The car seemed to buzz with electric silence. There was too much to say but no courage to speak.

Grandpa finally looked up in the rear-view mirror at me. Gran took his hand and sighed. The talk I had been waiting hours for was about to happen. I just felt like it would take too long to start it now.

"Honey…" Gran paused, as if unsure of how to speak to me. It was nothing new. Yet, here she was, about to give me my explanation far too late.

"We think this is the best thing for you. This institution has a high success rate," she said, clearing her throat. "Please don't hate us because we are trying to help you," she said, her last words lingering with me.

"Of course that's what you're worried about," I muttered. "It wasn't me. Isn't that enough for you? I'm telling the truth." Grandpa's eyes caught mine in the mirror. The look in his eyes said that he really wanted to believe me but he averted his eyes before I could catch a glint of hope in them.

Sighing, Gran stepped out of the vehicle and came around to my door. She opened it and I stepped outside into the bleak fall air. Tree's loomed overhead, displaying beautiful shades of orange, red and yellow. The lawn of the facility was manicured and bright green, even in mid-fall.

"Don't do this," I pleaded. "There's more too this than you know."

Gran forced a smile that looked more like a grimace, as if half-hoping I was right. She looped her arm into mine and started to walk to the double doors.

I turned toward her, walking to keep up. "I don't know how to tell you this, but Alana set me up," I cringed, realizing how crazy that really did sound. "No, I don't mean that, I mean she's dead but-" I stopped mid sentence in abrupt silence. The look on Gran's face was too much to take. I had said the wrong thing. Her face crumpled, as if all hope was gone. That was when I realized it was probably best to keep my mouth shut. It was always best. It was a wonder why I even tried anymore.

The steps of the facility loomed toward us, seeming to dull every thought in my mind. I was scared. I had no idea what to expect. All I could see from the outside was a relatively normal institution.

We entered the building, my heart pounding through my throat. We were greeted with health techs that lead me away, gently, as if they were scared that I might snap if they were too hands on. Which might have been my reaction if they had touched me. Turning around, I watched as Gran started to fill in mounds of paperwork. The door shut behind me and I continued to peer through the glass of the door, searching.

Gran turned and looked when she heard the door shut. When our eyes met, I saw nothing in them; they were cold and emotionless. They were accusing and empty. Because in her eyes, I had killed her perfect grandchild.

Robeline - Holes

Robeline seemed silent for the first time in a long time after I had poured out my story to her. She stared at me as if expecting more but I had nothing more for her.

Shuffling my feet, I started to smack the sole of my shoe against the floor. I remembered that it annoyed Robeline so I stopped as suddenly as I had started.

"I find your story very interesting," Robeline murmured, folding her hands on the tabletop. "It's very insightful. I can begin to understand what circumstance you were raised in and how it affects you now. I also feel like there are holes in the story," she concluded, folding her hands on the tabletop and peering at me with her beady eyes. "Do you have black-outs?" Robeline asked. "Time that just disappears on you?"

Sitting up straight in the chair, I cocked my head to the side, "Why would you ask that? If you want me to fill you in, then give me the time frame."

"When you dodge a

question, you're only answering it more clearly," Robeline said.

I didn't move. It took all my strength not to start screaming. I didn't even know why I had the urge to.

Robeline wrote something down and then looked up at me. "I don't understand why you didn't see Matt anymore after the kiss," she paused, "It just seems hard to believe because I can see that you're really…" she paused, "a *go-getter*."

Sighing, I rolled my eyes and gathered my thoughts. "The kiss was an accident. It was what got me in here in the first place. And it wasn't like Matt was into me anyway."

"How did Matt rejecting you make you feel?" she asked, putting her pen to her notebook.

I thought back to the feeling, the anger, and the hurt. "It made me feel like I wasn't good enough, once again," I admitted. "Maybe it's because I don't have blue eyes," I sneered, barking a humorless laugh.

Robeline didn't comment. "Do you think he has a specific type?" She asked.

"Yeah and it's not me," I muttered. "I'm not naturally blonde or blue eyed or perfect for that matter."

"But that's not why you dyed your hair blonde, or is it?"

Robeline asked.

Scowling, I fiddled with my hair, almost annoyed at her blatant straightforward question. "I dyed it because it looks good. And I had to fix my hair. It was time for a change." I glared at her.

Robeline nodded, apprehensive.

Alana – Dwindling away

I was drifting, like I was in a dream-like state. It was easier to blame that feeling on the fact that I was leaving this plane. It was too late to change anything and it was time to move on.

Fall was starting to dwindle away. Everything was dead. The grass was dead. It crunched under my feet. It was no longer green and lush. It seemed to bend over the edges of my shoes and prick at my feet as if I were allergic. As if I was still alive to feel irritation.

I was looking down at the ashes at my feet and remembering the building that used to stand in the place of the mounds of ashes. Looking into them, I searched for answers. Something had brought me back to this place. I just didn't know what.

The crunching of another person entering the forest, heading straight for me, shattered the silence. I looked toward the sound, wondering who I would encounter.

Matt. Some part of me already knew who it was but it still seemed to wind me, seeing him come towards me. My memories were flooding back now. I remembered the chase, the look in his eye. Memories I never thought would return poured into my mind. He was capable of so much more than I thought. It takes a lot to know someone inside out but I thought I knew him better than this. He looked up, his eyes making direct contact with me, which was enough to make my breath still in my throat.

"Matt? Why are you here?" I demanded, my voice shaking.

"I came to see you," Matt murmured. "And about the other day... I was struggling."

"What are you talking about?" I demanded, taking a step back.

Matt came at me head on, forcing his mouth on mine and making me melt in a second. Although I knew he was dangerous, I couldn't seem to pry myself out of his grip. My body was like Jell-O.

Finally, I pried myself out of his grasp and took a step back. "Why?" I asked, searching in his eyes. "Why did you kill me?"

Matt shook his head, as if confused by what I had said. He didn't answer me.

"WHY?" I screamed, my anger flooding into me harder and faster than I knew possible. It wasn't right for him to get away with my murder, to play it off like it didn't happen. He should be responsible for his actions.

"I didn't kill you," Matt murmured, stepping back, as if shocked by my forceful anger.

Taking a deep breath, I shook my head, blonde hair falling around my face. It was obvious he wasn't going to admit it. "I understand I did a lot of horrible things, Matt, but you killed me, and you were the person I trusted the most," I snapped, tears brimming my eyes. "For god's sake, at least I was openly awful. How could you do this to me? How do you go about *murdering* someone?"

Matt shook his head, hair falling into his eyes. "It wasn't like that," he stammered as if finally understanding what I was saying. Finally his eyes held an ounce of remorse, which was all I was looking for in my passing. After all of this time, I saw it.

"Then go ahead, Matt, enlighten me," I dared, holding back tears. "Clearly I have no idea why my murder was justifiable. So go ahead."

Matt stared at me, his eyes holding so much sorrow. He shook his head vehemently. "I don't know where to begin," he whispered. "Don't you remember?"

I shook my head, still in disbelief of him admitting it. Part of me wanted him to deny it. Part of me wanted it to be someone else.

243

"No Matt, I don't remember my own death, please fill me in." Tears spurting from my eyes and rolled down my face.

Matt shook his head, his eyes narrowing into me. "You killed her."

My heart dropped into my stomach, my mouth went dry. Even though what he had just told me had made no sense whatsoever it seemed to ring so true. "I killed me?" I asked.

"No, you killed your sister," Matt was crying now, his face crumpling like a used napkin. I had never seen him cry before.

"I am ALANA," I screamed abruptly. Looking down at my hand, I noticed that my fingernails were bitten down and bare. "Aren't I?" I cried, stepping back in alarm. Grasping my face I started to lose it. My hair. My hair was the same color as it was. I am Alana, I repeated to myself. I am. Alana. "I am Alana," I whispered to myself. Gripping my hair harder I started to pull at it.

"No, you are Ivy," Matt shook his head. "You killed Alana."

Robeline – The answer

"It was time for a change, but why now? Weren't you content with your life at one point?" Robeline asked.

I shook my head, "I was never content with my life."

"It doesn't add up," Robeline said. "It seems like that part of the story died at a dead end. What part did Matt have in this?" Robeline asked, tilting her head. "Where is the pivotal point in this? Where is the a-ha moment?" She squinted hard at me. "Where does everything go downhill?"

"Me being here is pretty much 'down hill', wouldn't you agree?" I asked, tilting back in my chair. "Isn't this 'pivotal' enough for your a-ha moment?" I was done explaining my feelings and getting a textbook response as to how I was feeling. I was done talking about Matt and I was done with the uncomfortable chair I had been sitting in for far too long.

Robeline didn't break eye contact, instead she folded her hands on the tabletop. "I'll admit that your whole story is a downward spiral," Robeline murmured. "I can't help but sense that Matt has more of a part in this story then you're letting on."

"He doesn't," I stated firmly. It was as if I was too used to hearing that accusation; too used to answering it in the same way.

Robeline shook her head, her dark eyes burning into mine. "From your story, I know he has a part in this Ivy, I think it's time for you to tell me."

"Matt had nothing to do with it." I gritted my teeth and gripped a strand of blonde hair, pulling it to the front of my face and examining the split ends. "The conditioner sucks here, you know," I muttered, pulling at the white ends that were about to split. "I need a lot of conditioner for my hair."

When I looked up, Robeline was staring at me, her lips pressed in a thin line. She was thinking, gathering information from my thoughts and my actions and my actions seemed distant and self absorbed, which would get charted.

"I didn't mean to change the subject," I murmured, combing my hand through my hair one last time. "It's constructive criticism, you can write that down."

Robeline shook her head, "I think conditioner would be that last concern for this place. Keep in mind, this place is to heal mind's, not prevent split ends," Robeline said, her tone cool.

Shocked by her abrupt come back, I sat back in my chair that wobbled from the shifting of my weight. "I don't know what to tell you," I said, blinking down at my feet. "I don't know how to make this make sense because even I don't know what the hell happened." I blinked at my tears that were welling in my eyes. I was beginning to look weak.

Clearing my throat, I looked up at Robeline. "I don't know what the fuck is wrong with me," I said in a clear voice. My hands were starting to shake.

"And that's why you were reluctant," Robeline murmured, "You didn't fight your grandparents on coming here, there is a part of you that wanted to seek help," she observed aloud, the gears in her head seemed to spin.

Nodding, I looked down at the ground. "The sad part is I really don't know what went wrong, what lead me here, and what the hell happened."

"To begin, we can start with Matt," Robeline pried.

"What the hell is with you and trying to find out about Matt?" I demanded, my voice booming through the room at a higher octave then I intended. "Why are you obsessed with him?"

247

Robeline shook her head and tightened her ponytail at the top of her head, as if flustered by my outburst of anger. It was obvious I was making her uncomfortable. She cleared her throat, "Why do you react in anger, Ivy?"

Looking out the window, I noticed the snow was coming down hard now. It was falling in fluffy clumps to the ground. Tugging on my sweater, I rolled up my sleeves.

Although it was so cold out there, it was seemed way fucking hotter in here. It felt like I was suffocating in the blaring heat of her little cubicle. It could have been the rage that I was digging up from the past. Nonetheless, the heater continued to click from the vents.

"Why don't you shut that thing off, isn't it hot enough in here?" I demanded, ignoring her question point blank.

Silence rang through the room. It seemed like my voice was so loud now. It didn't sound like me. Straightening up, I crossed my legs in more of a lady-like fashion.

"You didn't answer my question," Robeline pressed.

Gridding my teeth back and fourth, "Because I don't remember. I'm forgetful."

"Ivy," Robeline started, "I really don't think you can chalk this up to blatant forgetfulness. I think there's a bigger issue here. You *can't* remember. There's a reason why. There is always a reason why. The human brain is complicated but there's an answer."

"What are you talking about?"

"I believe I can joggle your memory if you let me, but please keep in mind that what I have to say is pretty… disturbing, especially from your point of view. Accepting it is the first road to recovery and it is my job to help you," she paused, waiting for my response.

Shaking my head I looked down at my feet. "I'm ready," I muttered. I wasn't.

Robeline looked down at her notebook, as if buying time to look me straight in the eye. That was when I sensed that what she had to tell me wouldn't be good. Hell, I knew all along it wouldn't be good. "Psychoanalysis takes years, Ivy, I can only tell you what I have gathered so far."

My back stiffened against the hard back of the chair, "Tell me."

Robeline blinked and shuffled her papers before leaning forward in her seat, the creaking of her chair echoing. "First off, I want to let you know that sometimes things happen in life that don't always make sense, but I want you to know that you are not alone in this and that we can and will treat this, however long it may take," Robeline started. She took a deep breath. "This might be difficult to hear, but from my observation, there's a chance that you have Dissociative Identity Disorder, otherwise known as Multiple Personality Disorder. When you gave me 'Alana's' side in your story, it was all in your mind. 'Alana' woke up in the shed with her hands and feet bound together which was a partial memory of her that you remember. When she escaped all she saw around herself was the ash and rubble that the shed had turned into which means you were struggling to see the vividness of your memory but it had clashed with reality. You were likely transitioning at this stage. This was the 'awakening' of your split personality, 'Alana.' Now in this case, there is usually a trigger to awaken this inside you. The trigger was seeing Matt and Angela together. You were infatuated with him and it set you off, yet you put it off as a moral issue and it 'awakened' your sister so-to-speak. It only escalated from there.

"When 'Alana' apologized to you for being cruel to you… That was a hope, that wasn't reality. 'Alana' was your conscience, but in a different personality altogether. 'Alana' said she didn't kill Angela because she was trying to help you see the truth. She wasn't lying; she was a partial angelic figure to you. The other half of

'Alana' was the cruel and awful one that bullied you, but she had good means, because the only time 'Alana' made you cry was when you kissed her boyfriend, which was morally wrong to you but something you craved for so long and you didn't know how to see it, you were completely disconnected from yourself. The night Alana died was the night that you began to change. You couldn't take the fact that you killed your own sister, so you tried to suppress it but failed. In order to suppress it entirely, you created your alter, Alana. So Alana killed herself in your mind. Your alter was created to help you deal with reality, to absorb everything you did wrong and everything you were going to do wrong so it didn't fall on you. You couldn't take what you had done..."

"Did you notice that 'Alana' apologized so much and tried to repair things with you because that was your subconscious trying to repair what you had done. You were apologetic for your actions, which is understandable from where you're at. Ivy, you created your own reality because you couldn't deal with life. You didn't know who you were and that was why you couldn't tell me anything about yourself. It wasn't that you didn't want to talk about it; it was that you didn't know. Alana would have never apologized to you, would she-?" Robeline paused, a look of pity in her eyes.

I didn't want her pity; it angered me. "You don't know what you're talking about," I accused, shaking my head. I started to blink tears away. I didn't know why I couldn't stop it.

"Ivy, your childhood was a mess of you feeling left out for being different and after feeling like you weren't good enough for so long. You began to let go of who you were and turned into something that you weren't. Your family didn't help. Alana was the 'princess,' her values, opinions, ideas; beauty was worth more than you were. It started at a young age. It developed slowly from there. Eventually, you couldn't take suppressing all of your bad memories through childhood and through your initial snap, that is why your alter came through when it did. Alana did bully you. I could tell from how you explained your interactions with her, and how you acted towards her. You were resentful and hateful towards her. And although your family may not have seen it, Alana was given the upper hand, she was the one whom your parents and grandparents *gloated* over. And because of that, Alana turned into your role model, you loved her and she had something that was special about her that drew you to believe that that was ideal," Robeline drew in a deep breath and paused, looking up at me. "Everyone around you lead you to believe that as well."

"That doesn't…" I stopped and shook my head. "No," I managed, my voice shaking.

"That's why you dyed your hair," Robeline continued.

"No," I repeated. My foot found the flap on the bottom of my shoe. Ripping at it, it began to come loose.

"That's why you started using your sisters makeup and her clothes," Robeline stated, her voice getting louder with my defiance.

"SHUT UP!" I screamed, my hands flying to my ears. "JUST SHUT UP!"

"Matt told you this when you were in the woods as Alana," Robeline continued, her voice stern and not letting up. It shattered through my skull. "Symptoms include insomnia, illusions, depression, mood swings – which explains how quickly your anger can take over. As well as substance or alcohol abuse…"

"I don't have a drinking problem," I snapped, shaking my head. Again, my foot peeled at the opening of my shoe, pealing at it, pealing at it, and pealing at it. Finally it tore completely off.

Robeline cocked her head to the side as if to tell me that she already knew I did. "You have gotten violently ill several times all at once, half of your story involves alcohol. When you were crying in the bathroom, what did you want more than anything? Alcohol." she answered her own question, shutting me down in my tracks. "Remember all of those times you saw Alana? Those were psychotic visual and auditorial hallucinations." Robeline paused and gathered more information to convince me.

"Every aspect of your attitude changed. You were never a 'go-getter' in the beginning were you? You were shy and reserved. You adopted every aspect of Alana, you used her mug, you started to drink coffee, you started partying, and all of the sudden you were hanging out with your sister's friends and you even kissed her boyfriend. When 'Alana' began to forget what she looked like... that was you forgetting her exact shade of blonde, the brightness in her blue eyes. She had been gone for so long that all of the little things about her were beginning to slip away from you and you tried to hold onto them to keep her alive in you. You thought that the Alana limbo that you had created was close to dying, except its interesting that you genuinely believed that you were Alana, you adopted the pain of everyone moving on without you from the misery of having no one to turn to.

"It only got worse from there. You weren't getting any love or respect from your grandparents so you dove into it, and it made you feel like a different person, a better person. Little did you know that your grandmother was getting suspicious of your behavior because she had overheard you talking to "Alana." She called in because she was worried about you, she saw the changes too she just didn't know what to do about it. We told her to bring you in immediately to have you assessed." Robeline took a deep breath and shook her head, continuing before I had a chance to say something, to question what I already seemed to know.

"Of course you didn't feel any better with all of the changes, you were still stuck in depression because the problem was bigger than you had originally thought. So naturally, you started to investigate your sister's murder and you started to place blame on everyone else around you like Angela, Tanya, Keith and even Matt. You were hiding from yourself, who you were, and what you did."

Shaking with anticipation, I stood up, the chair grinding on the floor behind me. Tears were streaming down my face full on. Ashamed, I wiped them away. I turned for the door but realized I had wrecked my shoe. In a flood of anger, I tore off both shoes.

"Accept it, Ivy. It's the fastest road to recovery." She realized I was starting for the door.

"Please, stay." Robeline threw herself forward and gripped my wrist. She looked down at it as if in shock that she had grabbed me. She released her grip the moment my eyes turned on her.

"Please," she pleaded. "Tell me what happened."

"If I could, I would," I said.

"Let me put you under hypnosis, don't you want to know what happened with your sister?"

Of course I did.

Ivy – Back to the party – (three months ago)

Robeline brought me to a different room with a video recorder in the corner and orange walls. The room was pretty much bare other than the couch and the chair across from it. I questioned the color of the room, it seemed a little too warm, like a cover-up for something. Other than the blaring heat, it was a lot nicer than the last room. It seemed as though the heat was the flaw of the entire building. I was just happy to finally leave the cubicle-room.

"Just lay down and try to clear your mind," Robeline said, nodding towards the brown leather couch against the wall.

Shaky, I did as she told me. I didn't want to talk anymore, I didn't want to hear anymore about my diagnosis. Then again, I did. There was too much guessing. I needed to know for sure what I had done and why I couldn't remember.

"Our main goal tonight is to get some clarification as to what happened the night your sister went missing. There's more to your disorder than that. There is also childhood trauma that we will have to keep working on sorting out and getting through. I assume most of it has to do with the bullying. But the main purpose of this session is to know what happened to Alana."

"W-what happened to Alana? Why would I know?" I asked, my voice shaky and meek.

"We don't know yet but if we can find something to close your sister's case then that is what we will do," Robeline said, clicking on the camera. She flashed me a reassuring smile and sat down on the seat across from me.

"Okay Ivy, we're going to count to ten. By the time I get to ten you will be back to that night and you will tell me step by step what is happening."

I nodded and swallowed the lump in my throat.

"Clear your mind. One. Two, you're drifting, three... four, five. Six, you're almost there. Seven, eight, nine, you remember, ten, you're there."

~

My mind was swimming as I watched Matt open the gate and push Alana out of the yard. I continued to down the rest of my drink while watching passively. The party was growing louder inside but I couldn't seem to peel my gaze from the window.

The sizzling of something on the stove made me turn around. A small group of people were arguing over ingredients to add to whatever they were cooking.

My eyes fell upon my tie-dyed bag across the room. I stumbled towards it. Ripping open my bag, I rummaged through it until I found my phone. I clicked on the screen and looked at the time, 11:43. It was getting late.

Looking up, I was face-to-face with a red haired girl. "How do you like your eggs?" she asked.

Distracted, I stood up on my toes to look around her. It was the awkward way to say I didn't want to talk to her. Since I was drunk, it was hard to hide how antisocial I really was.

"Um," the girl said, turning her head towards her friends and then laughing in unison with them.

"No eggs for you then," another girl chimed in from the stove.

"That's fine," I muttered, pushing past the girl and going back to the window. I pressed my face against the cool glass, trying to catch the awkward angle that I could see them at after they moved.

Butterflies whirled in my stomach as I watched Matt push

Alana to the ground. As I witnessed this, I didn't feel bad; I felt nothing other than a sense of satisfaction.

I watched Alana scramble back onto her feet. All I could do was stand and watch. *Sure, Alana. I'll stay out of your life,* I thought internally.

Matt started to lead her into the woods, stopping only to look behind him.

Spinning around, I noticed a few people staring at me.

"I'm feeling sick. I think I had too much to drink, maybe some fresh air will help," I announced, avoiding eye contact. Nobody said anything.

Panicked that Alana and Matt were leaving my sight, I scrambled out the door after them.

Straining my eyes, I looked towards the direction they walked in. They were headed further into the woods, I would have to catch up.

I slipped through the gate and jogged towards them. Their voices were loud through the quiet night.

"I don't want to do this," Matt said, his voice aching with pain, as if he were being forced to attack Alana. I struggled to quiet my heavy breathing and listen.

Alana's soft voice broke through, "then don't, please, we can work through this, I really do love you," she said, her voice cracking with emotion. It was one of the few times I had ever heard my sister cry.

There was a shocking amount of silence and then a scream that echoed through the forest, "STOP LYING TO ME!" Matt yelled. At that, Alana took advantage of the situation and ran. It seemed like time stopped as Matt tried to gather the remnants of his emotional relapse. He started to sprint after her, leaving my sight.

Jogging after them, I dodged tree limbs and stumbled over exposed tree roots. I caught up to them fast. Matt was only a stride behind Alana when I finally spotted him. He body checked Alana down onto the ground with impeccable force.

Alana was heaving into the ground, gasping for air. When she caught her breath she was crying, hard. It was something I had never witnessed before and it seemed unreal. Alana didn't cry, yet here she was crumpled on the ground, getting the beating of a lifetime. And here I was, unable and unwilling to stop it because I just didn't care and I couldn't seem to help it. I could only watch in shocked horror. My remorse for Alana had completely diminished.

After a few prolonged seconds, Matt picked Alana up by her

waist. Alana's crying didn't stop. She seemed to give into her fate now, not even bothering to look for an escape route.

"Move," Matt demanded, shoving her between the shoulder blades. Alana did as she was told and stumbled back into the woods, towards the shed that they had passed and I was crouched by. Staying low to the ground, I watched as Matt pushed Alana into the shed and shut it behind him. I figured the show was over. Matt wouldn't do much more than he already had.

In shock, I walked back to Tanya's and slipped through the back gate, the exact way I had gotten in. I was conflicted with what I had just seen and it haunted my mind every few seconds, but I went back to the party and started to drink my face off.

I was feeling like eggs anyway.

Six drinks and 3 shots in and I was feeling light on my feet, almost floating. My eyes caught the bright light on the stove that read 1:09. It seemed to blink through my mind as if giving off a warning. The party was dead. People were passed out in the living room. It was time to go home.

I clicked off the blaring music from the speakers. The house fell silent.

I went to the window, half hopeful of my sister's return. I

replayed what I had seen. The anger twisted on Matt's face. The way he pushed Alana to the ground. What I had seen had been far beyond what I thought Matt was capable of. But it wasn't any of my business. Or maybe I felt that way because it was Alana. Either way, I wasn't going to intrude.

It was late and it was time for me to head home and maybe check to see that Alana was alright, if I felt like it. Stepping out into the crisp summer night air, I drank in the smell of pine needles that lingered in the air. I moved forward through the gate in a drunken slumber, stumbling over the odd clump of moss. It would be easier to walk through the woods to get to my house. It was how I had gotten to Tanya's house without being seen.

That's when I saw the light. It was dim and barely visible in my wavering, drunken sight, but it was there nonetheless. The light was coming from the shed further back in the trees. I had always thought that shed was creepy and now there was candlelight coming from the cracks of the rotting 2 by 4's. It was a strange place to light a candle. I wondered if Matt and Alana were still in there. The thought made a shiver roll up my spine.

A newfound courage pushed me forward towards it. The dreaded thought that kept running through my mind was that it was

Alana. It was Alana and this was my fault. I crept closer and strained to hear something.

Muffled groans came from inside the shed. It sounded like someone was gagged in there. My first thought was that Alana was being raped inside. My neck pricked at the thought. Time to go, I realized, stumbling back through the path I had just came through. I had left just in time.

The cabin door swung open. Whoever was in there had heard me. Falling to the ground, I held my breath and counted. 1…2…3… The door shut behind the figure. All I could see was a dark shadow. My heart pounded through my body, coursing blood through my fingertips and making them tingle. Shuffling forward on the needle bed, I squinted toward the cabin, desperate to make out a face. All I could see was a mess of blonde hair. Matt.

Except his face was pale and ghastly. He looked disheveled, his clothes messed up from what looked like a struggle. His shirt was hanging in shreds at the bottom of his shirt. I couldn't even begin to piece together the scenario he had gotten himself into.

I breathed out a sigh of relief as he started to leave. Just as I was about to get up, my instincts told me not to. A tortured, muffled scream escaped from inside the cabin making my muscles twitch in fear. Settling flat against the ground, I held my breath.

Matt took a quick look around, his eyes seeming to linger where I was hiding. Holding my breath, I buried my face into the ground, too scared to move. The rancid, earthy smell of moss rose up in my nostrils. I hoped to god I wouldn't sneeze. I didn't hear him advance towards me.

Lifting my head up, I caught the sight of him almost out of view, running away from the scene. Once he was out of sight, I ran towards the cabin. Stepping through the tree roots and tiny shrubs, I finally reached the webbed up shed. Peering through the rotting wood I saw long light hair in the candlelight.

I rushed to the door and threw it open. It was Alana. Her hair was an unruly mess, showing the struggle that she had been through with Matt. Her mouth was gagged with a piece of Matt's shirt and she was tied up on the bench-table. Part of me felt bad. That maybe I should have come for her sooner. Then again, I doubted she would ever do the same for me, so what did it matter.

Alana looked at me, a blank look on her face as if she didn't realize she would be saved. And then she rolled her eyes in exaggeration, as if it was a shame I had to be the one to rescue her. As if she were waiting for someone better. "Sorry I wasn't somebody else," I heard myself say.

Rolling my eyes, I walked to her side. "Clearly you were waiting for someone better. Maybe Keith. But he was too preoccupied with his sick *girlfriend*," I muttered absently.

I noticed a glinting knife on the floor. Picking it up, I flipped it over in my hands. It was a long bladed knife with a tarnished silver handle. Heavy in my hands, I noticed it was made of steel. The edge was sharp to the touch. There was no reason it should be in here unless Matt...

"Did he threaten you with this?" I asked Alana. She thrust herself forward in the ropes as if frustrated that I had yet to cut her out. "Sorry," I said aloud, snapping back to reality.

But it was funny. How seeing her tied up like this had given me a sense of satisfaction. She didn't have the upper hand this time. She couldn't insult me. She was the helpless one for the first time.

Realizing how messed up those thoughts were, I shook my head. Easing the knife to the gag at her mouth, the knife cut through the fabric with ease.

"Seriously, what the fuck is wrong with you, I could've been murdered and all you're doing is fucking talking to yourself and swaying back and fourth like a drunken idiot. What were you thinking when you told Matt - were you trying to ruin my life?" She demanded, her eyes flaring.

Opening my mouth the answer her, I decided against it.

"Oh that's right, you have to get involved in everything in my life. You have to jump in like a superhero. You have no idea how he treated me! Knowing you, you're probably happy that I got a beating, aren't you? Fuck you. Get me out of here," Alana rambled, scowling and writhing her arms against the ropes.

I held the knife a little tighter in my grasp, the metal cold against my hand.

"What the fuck," Alana snapped, her voice cutting into my thoughts, she glared at me, her eyes cold. "Cut these off me, you idiot!"

"I'm not an idiot," I answered, the handle of the knife bit into my palm. It burned warm against my skin the longer I pressed it into my palm. "I'm not an idiot," I breathed to myself, my lungs constricting and refusing the air. It was like I was drowning again. The feeling that I would constantly get around her, only it wouldn't subside. Squeezing my fists, I tried to contain the anger that was bursting out of my chest and up my throat. Contain it; *contain it*. Breathe. JUST *BREATHE*.

"WHAT-" Alana barked but was interrupted by a look of alarm. I looked down at my left hand. It was plunged to her chest. I was holding the knife still, it seemed to sear against my skin. A wash of relief exuded through my body, the feeling of release. I pulled out the knife and then slammed it back into her body, anger radiating through me and making all of my hands numb with satisfaction.

I inhaled sharply, my head light from the sudden flow of oxygen.

And then it was as if a reality switch flicked on. Realizing what I had done, I stumbled back in shock. All I saw was red. All I felt was the heat of the blood. I looked down at my hands in disbelief. Red. Everything was red.

Choking on my breath, I gasped in horror at the scene in front of me. Alana started to choke on flowing scarlet blood.

"Alana!" I screamed in a desperate attempt, my hands flying up at my face, then down at her torso where I had stabbed her moments ago. The warmth of her blood radiated on my forehead where her blood remained. So much blood. Gasping and looking around the room, my shock turned to horror as her eyes shifted away from me and up to the ceiling, a thin glaze across them.

I would never be able to bleach my mind of this.

"Alana, no!" I shouted, "Stay with me!" I collapsed at her side, peering into her lifeless eyes hopelessly waiting for something to light up in them, anything to show that she would be okay. I could tell it was too late; I was too late. Stale blue replaced the light in her irises. She was gone.

Gasping for air, I slammed against the wall and sobbed. Sliding down the wall of the shed, spider webs and slivers of wood caught on my clothing and dug into my skin. All I could smell was damp, rotting wood and the raw smell of blood.

I stayed too long at Alana's side, hoping to god she would move. I glanced around the shed, frozen in shock, as the hours passed.

The sun was beginning to rise. A crack in the wall illuminated through the shed as my eyes shifted. The light seemed to knock me out of the shock.

I pressed my face against a crack in the wall. The sun was a bloody scrape emerging from the horizon, radiating brighter with every second.

Turning my attention back to Alana, I grasped her cool hand. "I'm sorry," I whispered, staring into Alana's lifeless eyes one last time, "I'm so sorry."

The door flew open. Matt. I jumped to my feet and dropped Alana's hand. He walked in, surveying the area in silence. Suddenly, I was unable to move, unable to speak, unable to breathe. My body started to shake in tremors.

"Matt," I managed, shaking my head vehemently. I struggled for words, choking on anything I tried to say because it wasn't enough. Finally I managed, "It wasn't me." I didn't know what I meant by that but it sounded true. It couldn't have been me.

"What the hell do you mean it wasn't you?" Matt cried. His face crumpled as he stumbled closer. His eyes flickered between Alana's bloodied torso and the blood all over my hands and face.

"I-I don't know," I said, "please, I'm too young to go to jail for this." Tears sprung to my eyes and leaked down my cheeks. "Please. I can't take the fall for this. I didn't mean to. My anger got the best of me," I looked at Alana's lifeless body on the bench table. Blood had tainted what seemed like every square inch of the place.

My words didn't seem to register. The only thing Matt could look at was Alana. His hands fell to the knife in her torso. "What did you do?" he screamed, causing me to shake. He turned paper-white and started to tremble, his eyes refusing to waver from Alana's cold body.

270

I looked down at my blood stained hands for an answer. I didn't have one. Heavy tremors racked through my whole body, they turned into heaving sobs. It happened too fast. But even that wasn't an excuse. Collapsing to the floor, I murmured incomprehensible gibberish, as I tried to piece everything together.

Matt was on his knee's at Alana's side, holding her limp hand between his. He pressed his index finger to her neck, feeling for a pulse. After what seemed like a full five minutes, he started crying as hard as I was.

"I don't know what to do," I said, tears streaming down my face. They were beginning to dry. The rancid air in the room made my face itchy.

Realization set in. Matt stood up as if he had suddenly made a decision. "Stand up," he ordered. I did as he said. He grabbed both sides of my face. "I'm going to need you to cooperate, do you understand?" He asked, his wide, blue eyes boring into mine. I shook my head. "We have to hide the body," he said, his voice shaking.

I shook my head no. More tears sprang to my eyes. "No, no, no," I shook my head, avoiding his penetrating stare.

"We don't have time to grieve right now, we have no other choice!" Matt said, his eyes pleading with me. He gripped my hands with his. "We can't get out of this." He shook his head, turning to Alana's body. "I'm screwed. You're screwed. We're both *screwed*. They're going to find both your fingerprints and mine all over this place. We have no other option. We don't have much time. Do you understand?" he asked. I have never seen such desperation in his eyes. It made me feel faint.

I nodded, but couldn't seem to gather my mind enough to think.

"Grab her feet," Matt ordered.

Trembling, I stumbled to her feet. Matt pulled the knife from Alana's body. Looking away, I swallowed the puke that lurched up my throat.

Matt looked over at me, concerned. "Are you okay?" he asked.

I nodded my head because it was all I could muster at that point. Matt turned his attention back to his work, he cut the ropes near my hands with the blood stained knife that I held only an hour ago before plunging it into my sisters' body. The ropes fell to the floor. I grasped her feet. Matt worked at cutting the rest of her body free.

"We're going to need to be quick," Matt said, his eyes

darting around the tiny shed.

"I'm still drunk," I whispered, tears pooling in my eyes again. I wiped them away with my red hands.

"Ivy, pay attention. We need to focus now. We have to get rid of the body and quick. The sun is going to rise soon and we will lose our future if we don't do this, I swear to god," Matt pleaded.

"Okay let's go," I said, finally snapping back to reality. *This isn't my sister, I didn't kill my sister,* I told myself repeatedly, while looking away from her body. We stumbled out the door and into the cool early morning air.

The woods were alive in the early morning. The air was cool and fresh, the pungent scent of pine wafted through the forest. Birds sang around us as we shuffled Alana out further toward Tanya's house where Matt's truck was parked. I could see it but it seemed so far away.

"We have to be faster," Matt groaned under the weight. The dead weight of Alana's small body was more than I imagined it would be. I watched the ground and was careful not to look at my dead sisters' body, it was more than I could stomach. We stumbled and tripped through the woods, slamming Alana's fragile body into tree limbs that were marked with her blood on impact. All I could think of was *evidence*; we were going to get caught.

We reached Matt's truck. He threw her body in the box of the black Chevy, and slammed the tailgate shut. He then ran to the cab of his truck and shuffled in the back for a moment, searching for something.

Looking around, my heart started to race.

After what seemed like a full five minutes, Matt emerged from the truck with a blanket. He threw it over her and tucked it under her, cringing as he touched her. It wasn't much coverage but we didn't have time. I watched in blind horror, frozen to the spot and unable to function.

"We don't have time to gawk," Matt stated, catching the look on my face, "Get in."

I jumped in his truck with shaky legs.

Everything in his truck was so normal, *too normal* compared to what had just happened. Country music blared through the truck as soon as Matt started the engine. Taking a deep breath, I tried to convince myself that what had just happened was only a dream. I could only wish.

The scarlet blood streaks had drenched through my jeans and coated my hands. I tried to rub the blood on my jeans, dizziness setting in. *Breathe,* I reminded myself. Matt drove about 20 minutes on a terrain road deeper in the forest. Over each bump in the road I was shaken back into reality. Every time, reality hit harder and harder. Finally we stopped.

Lightheaded, I stumbled out of the vehicle as he abruptly stopped the truck. I bent forward sharply, acid-like vomit lurching up my throat for the second time. After that, I vomited several more times. Choking and sputtering, I tried to regain my balance and stand up straight but the world seemed to be tilting.

"Ivy," Matt said. I felt his eyes baring into me. "We have to get this done. Please snap out of it. If we're going to get out of this we need to focus. Both of us."

Standing up, I wiped my mouth and cringed. Breathing hard, I walked toward him, my legs trembling with the beginning of an awful hangover.

"I need you at her legs again," Matt snapped, "Quick."

Hesitant, I grasped her legs and we began to haul her deeper into the forest.

After stumbling for several minutes we found a thick bush and Matt stuffed her body under it in a hurry. It hid her good enough. It would take a lot to find her and the woods were vast.

Although I felt a tinge of relief, I couldn't overcome the feeling of disbelief and horror of the events that had just occurred. Cold sweat started to pulse through my body as I stared at the bush in silence.

"We have to go," Matt said, his hand on my back.

Starting to cry again, I collapsed onto the forest floor. Dirt, leaves and twigs stuck to the dried blood all over my clothes and hands. Crying harder, I turned over and moved to a sitting position. I tried to peel the leaves and twigs off one by one. The dirt wasn't going to come off. All I could think of was that it wasn't just blood, it was *my sister's blood.*

All I could remember were all of the good times we had together no matter how scarce. I remembered the laughs, the fun, and the times we had together as little girls. But I destroyed her. I killed my own sister.

The longer I stayed on the ground, the more everything felt real. The sunrise illuminated the forest in a beautiful glow, revealing the secrets and the blood on the bark of the trees. I walked towards Matt. "We have to go."

"I know," Matt said, transfixed on the bush that my sister was in. Looking around, I looked for the drips of blood that lead a path to the bush. There were crimson marks on the trees nearby her corpse. It was so apparent to me but I knew it was going to be harder to notice for someone not looking for it. The blood would wash away with the next rainfall.

"We have to burn down the shed," I said aloud in realization. It was the one thing we had forgotten to do to clean up our mess.

Matt nodded, then started to walk toward the truck without another word. I followed him.

In his truck we listened to the music quietly. It felt like everything had changed because of the death of my sister but at the same time it felt like everything was the same and I was almost ashamed that nothing changed. The only difference was the emptiness I felt and the blood on my hands. It seemed like all of my emotions had gone numb as I tried to accept what had happened. It was hard for me to even believe. Everything felt like a dream. I hoped it was. The music droned on but conversation was dead. Crying in silence, I looked out the window, hoping Matt wouldn't look at me.

Matt stared ahead, ashamed of his tears but unaware of mine.

We arrived back at the shed and Matt dumped some gas from a gas can in the back of his truck all over the inside of the shed.

We were running out of time, I could tell by the sun peaking over the trees. We had to be quick. He struck a match. Threw it on. And just like that, the evidence of the horrors that I had caused went up into flames. The flames rose higher, flew up and raged toward the sky with the initial drop of the match and simmered down to a steady burn. Thick smoke billowed up to the sky, engulfing the sweet morning air with the rancid smell of rotten, burning wood.

"The knife?" I asked.

"We don't have time but we have to throw it in the river," Matt said. "For now, we're going to bury it."

"I'll take it," I offered. Matt looked at me under raised eyebrows.

"We don't have time to bury it right now," I motioned toward the light that was pouring through the trees now. "We have to get cleaned up or my grandparents will know I'm gone."

Reluctant, Matt nodded. He handed me the knife.

The cool metal seared against my skin, reminding me of the horrors that I had been through in the last six hours. I threw the knife in my bag.

"We'll never talk of this again," I heard myself say. A hot flash seized through my body, reminding me that the hangover was just beginning.

After grimacing at Matt as if it were some sort of goodbye, I started to stumble towards my house in a hurry and left him staring into the fire.

Crunching through the woods, I breathed in the fresh air and tried to convince myself that everything would be okay. It would blow over. Life would continue as it normally would… I just needed a shower.

I crept through the woods until I saw my house. Gran was sitting out with her coffee on the front porch. I continued to creep towards the back of the house. My biggest goal was to get inside without making my grandparents suspicious of my whereabouts. What they didn't know wouldn't hurt them.

I snuck in through the downstairs back door and ran to the washroom. As I took off my clothes, I examined the blood that had now dried to my skin. It made me queasy. I didn't want to think about what had just happened. Turning on the hot water full blast, I waited, examining my face in the mirror. My eyes looked bloodshot which was expected from not sleeping but there was something else in them, a look of shame and darkness. Peeling my gaze from the mirror, I stepped into the shower, the water shocking my cool skin on impact.

Running my bloodstained hands through my hair, I reached for the shampoo bottle and squeezed a blob of scented shampoo into my palm and forced it through my hair. The blood had made it into my hair and it seemed to hold onto the scent of the kill. I lathered over and over and over again. It wasn't enough. I squirted some shampoo on the floor of the tub. It mixed with the blood, leaving a scent of cucumber watermelon and the raw smell of blood. Holding onto a sob that was forcing its way to the surface, I squeezed the shampoo bottle upside down, the thick scent wafting to my nose. The smell nauseated me because it smelled even more like Alana. There wasn't any escaping what had happened only hours ago. I turned up the heat in the shower.

The scalding water did nothing for my shame like I thought it might. Although it burned, I didn't seem to care because I deserved it. I shouldn't care enough to turn it down. The feeling of scalding water would not measure to the feeling of a knife in the abdomen.

Bursting into tears, I fell into the puddle of water in the tub. Remembering the tub was nearly clogged, I cried harder in frustration. *I was bathing in my sister's blood,* I realized, standing up on wobbly legs. *Shake it off,* I told myself.

My mind started to spin with possibilities.

Alana would have thought that my crying was pathetic. She would have thought that I couldn't handle myself and that there was no way I could go on living. Alana would have handled this situation far better. There was no reason to feel guilty. If anything, she killed herself.

I didn't *really* kill my sister. She put herself in that situation. She had to have known what was coming. She must have. So really, Alana killed herself. It wasn't me. I didn't do it. Something seemed to ring true about that. Alana was reckless and childish - even stupid at times. She let it kill her.

It was only then that I started to think a little clearer. My heavy breathing slowed. Everything would be okay. It started slowly, as a leak in my mind. Then it started to click. It resonated with me and so it started to flood uncontrollably once I started to agree with the reasoning my mind was giving me. I was almost relieved that Alana was gone. She wouldn't be around to bring me down. I would no longer be compared to perfection. I, instead, could be perfection. I could be whatever I wanted to be because no one was standing in my way anymore.

Life would be easier. I would no longer feel like my lungs

were giving out around her.

So what I had done wasn't really all *that* bad. And I could block it from my mind if I tried hard enough. The blood was washed from my hands. Everything seemed normal. This was *normal.*

My sister had gone *missing, my sister was missing, my sister was missing.* I took a deep breath of hot steam and pressed my forehead to the wall in the shower as the hot water cascaded over me. Alana was just gone and it was all a dream. It was all a dream that I would soon forget. A giggle erupted from my throat as I watched the blood swirl down the drain.

And the sickening part? I felt like I could breathe again.

Robeline - Illusions

My eyes were wet with tears when I fell out of my trance. My hands were still shaking.

Robeline was reviewing notes. She moved her pen over her notebook and started to fill in line after line of my medical diagnosis. All I seemed to be able to read was *murderer murderer murderer*. It was all in my mind. Everything was all in my mind.

I sat up, my mind groggy. The one thing that I knew for sure was that I was the one who had plunged the knife into my sister. I guess I was good at blocking things out. The puzzle pieces were beginning to come together as I sat across from Robeline who was still writing feverishly.

Little things were starting to click, like the reason why Alana's shampoo sickened me and why we were out of shampoo. All because I was trying to hard to mask the scent of raw blood as I showered. That's why I had to buy new shampoo.

All of the times that I saw what I thought was my dead sisters ghost – it was really my mind all along. I looked down at my shaky hands. I imagined the blood that had coated my hands with my dead sisters blood. I imagined Alana's blood all over myself again.

"Integration has begun," Robeline stated, "You may remember bits and pieces here and there. It's a process. You're welcome to ask questions."

"So when I... Awakened as Alana... I awoke in the shed, I struggled to get out of the restraints. It felt so *real*."

"The shed was an illusion," Robeline answered me.

I thought back to the memory. It was different this time. I had snuck into Alana's room, after I found out about Matt and Angela. I put on a pair of Alana's cobalt stilettos. They were the only ones I could find that were similar to what she had woken up to that night. I remembered stumbling into the forest, wobbly for the first time in heels. It was early morning; the sun was barely a sliver over the horizon. I remembered falling to the ground on the forest floor, tracing the silver knife across my wrists, back and fourth, back and fourth. I relished the pain, even though I was careful to cut harder along the edges of my writs and not the middle. I remembered laying back in the remnants of the burnt down shed. I shifted that morning. I remembered the morning I had stayed with my sister's body until the sun rose, awakening me from my slumber. I took in the surroundings, creating a false world to store the pain. As I had strained against the ropes, I only slashed at my arms harder, blood streaming to my upturned palms. I lay back. My mind took over. And suddenly, a burden was lifted. I had split into two. Alana could take away my pain for the first time in my life. I let her have it because I couldn't take it anymore.

My gaze fell my scarred wrists. The scars were thick on the edges of my wrists. "I saw myself, I talked to myself..." I reasoned, "When I came back... After I showered, I talked to myself. That isn't possible."

"It was an illusion, you were playing both parts to that role."

The memory replayed in my head. I got out of the shower and put Alana's clothes back on. I saw myself as Alana. I left the washroom and glanced up at myself in the mirror. That was when 'I' showed up. In the memory, I was talking to myself in the mirror.

"When I left my room to talk to gran, Gran wouldn't respond," I said, my voice shaking.

"You were likely watching from across the room through a window," Robeline answered, "Tell me more about that incident."

"Gran walked through Alana... me. How can that be

explained?"

"It didn't happen, you likely imagined the interaction. However, you've always felt invisible to your grandmother. Keep in mind the fact that 'Alana' was supposed to take all of your pain. She felt it instead of you. When she walked through Alana, she ignored Alana. It could have been a delusion of how you felt."

How I felt. I acted based on how I felt, and it made me become the lead part in a horror story. Alana wasn't in my way anymore. I could finally be what I wanted to be. I took over Alana's life. I left my pain behind. I looked down at my shaking hands. I imagined the crimson that had coated my hands. My sister's blood. The image refused to go away. It was all I could see.

I couldn't take it. Even though all of my questions were answered, I couldn't believe it.

"W-who killed Angela?" I asked, my voice shaking.

Robeline set her pen down and then looked up at me. "Alana was jealous," Robeline said slowly, "It's safe to assume..."

"It was me," I whispered, shaking my head, tears spurted to my eyes. I was back in that memory. Back in Angela's quiet house, I felt the anxiety as my eyes met my own in the dark window across from the door. "I saw myself in the window," I thought out loud.

"That's why I dropped the knife." The knife clattered to the floor in the memory. It flashed forward to Angela, her face inches from mine. 'I was never your friend,' Angela said in the memory that replayed in my head. Her tone was harsh. It cut through me. 'In that case, this should be easier than I thought,' I replied, slamming the knife into her. Blood coated my hands again. I was transfixed by the color. I couldn't tear my eyes from it.

"I'm a killer," I murmured, tears dripping from my stiffening jaw.

Robeline nodded. "The first step is accepting what you have done wrong, accept all of the emotions, the good, the bad, and the ugly. We can move on from there,"

A heavier set health tech cracked the door open, he cleared his throat, "It's time for your next appointment." His green eyes flickered to me and then back to Robeline. He opened the door fully and stepped in, his expression turning when he noticed my torn up shoes and my bare feet. I had almost forgotten that I had completely destroyed my shoe. I must have looked crazy.

I wouldn't have judged his anxiety towards me; there were a lot of rumors as to why I was there. He was probably scared he would be my next victim. I didn't know how I felt about that. I might have felt empowered by that because it was better to be feared then to be invisible.

Standing up, I exchanged one last glance with Robeline.

"Thank you, Ivy, for your participation, we will work through this in your next session. We will get to the bottom of this," she paused, "actually, I think you'll be able to participate in the rest of family day if you're interested." She grasped my shoulder and squeezed it. She stood up and shuffled her papers.

"What makes you think they're even here?" I muttered to myself.

Robeline looked up at me, "they weren't here last family day?" She asked. She seemed to already know the answer as she shifted her eyes from me.

The apple in my throat seemed to suffocate me. I didn't know why I let it bother me anyway. What else was I really expecting? I guess there was a part of me that thought that there was something left.

"See you next session," I said, spinning around on my heel. I couldn't help but wonder if my diagnosis made any sense to her. Maybe she understood why I had to do what I did.

The people who I had killed weren't beloved characters in

my life; the Alana that I had killed was the one who deserved it. I had killed the evil in her. I don't have remorse for people and I don't have remorse for myself because you create your reality.

I was a good person. I took what I could for as long as I could. But I didn't deserve it. I deserved compassion, respect, love. Everything that I couldn't receive with her in my way. I had to help myself because if I didn't - who was going to? *I was a good person.*

The health tech lingered in the doorway. He stood to the side, waiting for me to walk through. I flashed a smile at him, content with the uneasiness that grew over his features.

I brushed past him, a smile spreading across my face. Out of the corner of my eye, I caught Alana's dashing smile.